Gail felt utterly alone.

I eased the receiver back on the cradle, and the minute—no, the second I took my hand away, the phone rang. It was almost supernatural. When the receiver was next to my ear again, it was still warm.

And there at the other end was the most terrifying voice I'd ever heard. Sometimes I still hear it, just as I'm going to sleep or in a room that's too quiet. It wasn't quite human. Neither male nor female. A high, hollow voice, someone crying out the words from the inside of a bell. Disguised, falsetto, almost like a child shrieking. But more controlled than that because I understood every word.

"ARE YOU IN THE HOUSE ALONE?"

There was a sobbing, whistling laugh. It was too terrible to be real. And too real to be a horror movie. If there'd been a hundred people in the house with me, all ready to defend the place, I'd still have been paralyzed.

And then that voice again.

"ARE YOU IN THE HOUSE ALONE?"

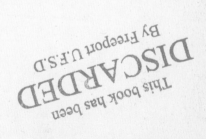

OTHER BOOKS BY RICHARD PECK

RICHARD PECK

Are You in the House Alone?

PUFFIN BOOKS

For Dr. Richard L. Hughes, who helped

PUFFIN BOOKS
Published by the Penguin Group
Penguin Putnam Books for Young Readers,
345 Hudson Street, New York, New York 10014, U.S.A.
Penguin Books Ltd, 27 Wrights Lane, London W8 5TZ, England
Penguin Books Australia Ltd, Ringwood, Victoria, Australia
Penguin Books Canada Ltd, 10 Alcorn Avenue, Toronto, Ontario, Canada M4V 3B2
Penguin Books (N.Z.) Ltd, 182-190 Wairau Road, Auckland 10, New Zealand

Penguin Books Ltd, Registered Offices: Harmondsworth, Middlesex, England

First published in the United States of America by The Viking Press, 1976
Published by Puffin Books,
a member of Penguin Putnam Books for Young Readers, 2000

10 9 8 7 6 5 4 3 2

Copyright © Richard Peck, 1976
All rights reserved

THE LIBRARY OF CONGRESS HAS CATALOGED THE VIKING EDITION AS FOLLOWS:
Peck, Richard. Are you in the house alone?
[1. Rape—Fiction.] I. Title.
PZ7.P338Ar. [Fic] 76-28810
ISBN 0-670-13241-1

Puffin Books ISBN 0-14-130693-9

Printed in the United States of America

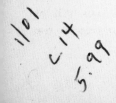

PROLOGUE

From the first warm night of spring until autumn, Steve and I would slip out to the Pastorinis' cottage on the lake, Powdermill Lake. How often? Ten times? Twelve? I don't remember now. I kept no diary. We left no clues.

All our fantasies, Steve's and mine, seemed to come true in that little dark corner of time. We thought that making love was being in love. I never wanted to imagine what might come next. That would have spoiled everything. The best part was the way we seemed to be absolutely alone together. And now I know we weren't alone out there at all. Someone was watching us, maybe every time.

We'd leave our clothes in a heap before the cold stove in the cottage. Then we'd bang back the screen door and pound down the sloping lawn to the pier, our footsteps rumbling on the boards like thunder. And then we'd dive into the lake.

I remember one October night when it was still as warm as August. I remember it because it was nearly the last time. There was sheet lightning over the Connecticut hills to the north, and the steamy mist rolled off the center of the lake. The surface of the water wrinkled with raindrops all around the white circle of Steve's head, and his arms wavered just below the surface. I stood with my toes hooked around the end of the pier, wet already from the rain. But I hung there, almost overbalanced, before I plunged into the black water.

For some reason I'd grabbed up my yellow slicker and held it over my head all the way to the end of the pier. Then I let it drop, and it collapsed there at my feet like a parachute. Steve floated farther out on his back, and I could see the length of his body luminous in the darkness. The lake was shallow a hundred yards out. It was always exciting, never dangerous. Before I dropped into the water, Steve called my name and laughed, waving me in.

My name, Gail, carried in waves across the lake and probably up above the treetops.

There was a big stand of rock up there, just above the cottage. It was like a watchtower, and the top of it was as flat as a table, weathered smooth. Everybody knew the path that led up to it. On clear nights sometimes Steve and I climbed up there to count the stars—or just to sit together, very close and quiet, pretending we could read each other's thoughts.

I wonder now if someone else was with us that night, standing up on the watchtower rock, hearing Steve call my name, watching me drop into the water and seeing us swim toward each other.

CHAPTER

One

Only the mighty Lawvers would give a dinner party for a bunch of high-school juniors. A real dinner party, with damask dinner napkins and finger bowls, with Lawver Mother at one end of the Duncan Phyfe table and Lawver Father at the other end. And two pairs of edgy sixteen-year-olds facing each other in between, across a bowl of stiff chrysanthemums.

Of course nearly everybody in Oldfield Village went to the Lawvers' Thanksgiving Day receptions. But for the rest of the year the Lawvers withdrew into their Old Settlers' Set.

While I was trying to get dressed for the ordeal, my mother was in and out of my room twenty times. On the last trip she was carrying an evening skirt of hers, jet black. "Gail, with a dressy blouse, maybe you could carry this off."

"Mother, I'm practically pulled together already. A non-dressy blouse with a V-neck sweater and a short skirt. Alison's wearing more or less the same. We worked it out.

And look, Mother, *stockings.*" I stuck out one leg at her.

"Well, at least you're not in Levi's," she said, still holding the evening skirt high. I'm not in Levi's any more than anybody else, but she had to say something. Finally she gave up, coming back only once to fire a zinger at me. "Better be downstairs when Steve gets here. It would *kill* him if he actually had to come in and carry on a civilized conversation with me and your father."

"All *right*, Mother." No time to get into Steve with her. I'd have met him on the corner if I'd had the nerve. And it wasn't even our own plan. The only reason we were going to the Lawvers was because of Alison.

I thought of her as my best friend then. Since she'd been going with Phil Lawver for two years, his parents had given in and decided it was time to Receive Her Socially. To be subtle about it, they told Phil to invite another couple, *any* other couple, probably. So Steve and I were appointed. Or maybe *summoned* is the word. "Do it for me," Alison had said. "Then I'll owe you a favor, and I won't forget."

I stood in front of the mirror, brushing my hair, waiting for all that body and bounce they promise you on the commercials. I was just getting past the phase where you still search the mirror expecting to surprise yourself with Sudden New Beauty. Instead, I just looked very very clean. Besides, my mother kept appearing in the mirror over my shoulder every two seconds, which is distracting.

When I couldn't think of anything else to do to myself, I started down the stairs. In the living room Mother's conversation was coaxing Dad out from behind the October *Architectural Record* magazine. She was all over the house that night.

If I sat down, quietly, on the third step from the landing,

I could look straight out through the fanlight window over the front door. That way I'd see Steve when he started up the walk and could pass the time eavesdropping on the living-room conversation. I was just beginning to see my parents as people once in a while, and not just as parents. This wasn't one of the times.

"Seems a bit—premature—to me," Mother was saying.

"What does?" Dad said.

"Lydia and Otis Lawver putting their stamp of approval on the Bremer girl. Now if she and Phil were already in college, and the whole thing looked inevitable—"

"Lydia and Otis Lawver never put their stamp of approval on anything," Dad said, trying to quell the conversation.

"You know what I mean. Of course, it's very nice—and gracious. I suppose we'd do the same thing if Gail was—seeing—a suitable boy."

"I hope we wouldn't do anything just because the Lawvers do it." Dad's voice sounded weary.

"I know we can't hope to copy the grandeur of people like them. And I don't suggest we try. After all, they are almost absurdly lofty. Still . . ." —

It would have been nice, I sat there thinking, if Dad had come to the rescue after Mother's crack: the one strongly implying that Steve wasn't a "suitable boy." There were even times when I suspected myself of going with Steve mainly to spite my mother. It was hard to keep a sense of proportion between them. I was never exactly sure whether I was acting or reacting. That was the kind of thing I worried about back then.

I saw Steve through the fanlight window, coming up the walk. But before I opened the front door, I reached inside my blouse and pulled up the chain with the little green heart on it, letting it dangle on the outside of my sweater. The stone heart Steve had given me.

"I know it's a Friday night, but come straight home!" Mother called from the living room. "I mean it now!"

Steve drew me out into the evening. We walked down the street, hand in hand, through spirals of autumn-smelling bonfire smoke. He hadn't gone all the way to a suit, but under a wool jacket he wore a white shirt and a tie. His dark hair curled down over the white collar.

"Do you mind going to the Lawvers'?" I said after a little while. "I know you and Phil haven't got a lot to say to each other."

"I'm not all that crazy about Alison either, as a matter of fact," he said. "But it's no big thing. My family's been going to the Lawvers' for years."

"You're kidding."

"Sure we have. We've been repairing the plumbing in that mausoleum of theirs for generations. Probably an early Pastorini put in the first flush toilet for an early Lawver."

"History's so fascinating," I said. "What did your family do for them before flush toilets?"

"Supplied them with chamber pots for under the beds, I guess. Your basic thunder-mug type with the big pink roses on them."

"Well, enough about history."

I meant it too. There was something feudal about Oldfield Village and all its smug snugness. All those old New England families living by their ancient codes like Pilgrims before we New York types moved in and turned it into a suburb. We seemed to have changed the town from a real place into a reasonable facsimile, all carefully restored down to the last gold-plated lightning rod.

Alison's family and mine had both moved up from New

York. But hers got here first. They arrived when she was in first grade because they were escaping the New York school system. And then the Bremers had "gone native," as people said. Her father gave up Wall Street and opened a paint and decorative-hardware store in the Village Center. So Alison really fitted in more than I did. Maybe that's where our friendship began. She knew her way around. I didn't. I wasn't a misfit, but I never could see Oldfield Village as the center of the universe.

We hadn't moved out of New York until I was ready for middle school. Then my dad commuted to his architectural firm in Manhattan. I never forgot our first autumn here. Dad wore his new glaring red plaid lumberjack shirt from Abercrombie and got a terrible case of blisters all over his hands from the first leaf-raking. I thought the village was on fire because everybody burned mounds of leaves as big as haystacks at the curbs. That was back when I was always at Dad's elbow, "helping" him, being his little girl, and maybe his little boy too. But I was a New Yorker born, and years later I could still feel city cement under my feet, even on the historic brick sidewalks of Oldfield Village.

I didn't really mind feeling I didn't belong one hundred percent. It wasn't just the old families rooted like ancient oaks. It was the school too, with everybody locked into little groups and branded like cattle. The heads were at the top, running the Student Council during the week and smoking joints on the weekend at Friendly's. And the rest of us in the middle all divided up into fairly straight little cells. Then down at the bottom, heads again—zombies in plastic leather.

Sometimes even before last fall I felt strangled by the place. Everything so neat and perfectly organized. On the surface.

Steve's hand tightened on mine when we got to the stone

gates of the Lawver place. When the house was already a couple of hundred years old or so, a Victorian Lawver had added a curving drive and a lot of trees—to screen the house from the town growing up around it. Steve called it a mausoleum. It was more like the world's largest barn, to house a family too self-confident to worry over the latest trend in Good Taste.

One dim lamp beside the flat front door winked light through the shrubbery. "Well, here we go," Steve said. "One serf and a barbarian approaching the moat. Wonder if they'll let down the drawbridge."

After he'd lifted the door knocker and let it fall with a crash, he ran his arm around my waist and started kissing me under the ear: a sort of tingling annoyance. He was still doing it when Phil Lawver opened the door, wearing a gray flannel suit that would carry him right on into Yale.

He was tall and athletic with ice-blue eyes. His hair was blond, slicked down and damp at the ends, as if he'd just stepped out of the shower after a squash game.

He was usually smooth in an absent-minded way, but the sight of us turned his face red. "Yeah, well, come on in. Ah . . . glad to see you."

He led us like a young lord through the big double parlors where the Thanksgiving reception was always held. We went past the wing chairs and the portraits of Lawvers all the way back to the time of black hats and buckled shoes. They were descended directly from the first Thanksgiving. And they'd always had plenty to give thanks for ever since.

The family, and Alison, were sitting in the room beyond that, a study with book shelves and a fire snapping in the hearth. It occurred to me that Alison planned to live in these rooms one day, stepping in to form a link with Phil in the endless chain of Lawvers. At the age when the rest of us were tacking up posters of David Bowie and Bruce Springsteen, Alison was sketching floor plans full of eighteenth-century furniture and giving china patterns serious thought.

She was sitting with the firelight on her face in a chintz-covered sofa beside Mrs. Lawver, nodding at her conversation. When I saw how Phil's mother was dressed, I was glad I hadn't given in to Mother's wardrobe suggestion. She stood up in a long black crepe skirt and a dressy blouse, along with a string of the family pearls.

Then she turned her cameo face to us and said, "Gail, how nice. How is your darling mother? I haven't seen her since the Women's Exchange benefit. And your father? That grueling commute every day! How awful for him!" She had one of those distantly echoing voices, coming to you from high atop a Connecticut hill.

Phil retreated behind the sofa from all this graciousness, bumping into his father, a shorter, rounder version of Phil. "And Steve—it is Steve, isn't it? How very nice that you could come." Mrs. Lawver put out a long white hand and gathered Steve into the circle.

They were like a family portrait in faded, muted colors. A painting of themselves in their own museum. *Study in Gray Flannel and Black Crepe.*

"Otis, come and meet these young people. Gail is the Osburnes' daughter. You know those people who have done such a sweet restoration of the old Milton house. Really very clever. Father's an architect.

"And this is the youngest Pastorini boy."

Mr. Lawver ambled forward and put out his soft hand. "Pastorini? Pastorini?" he said, "Aren't they the—"

"Yes, of course," Mrs. Lawver cut in smoothly. "And why don't you pour the young people glasses of tomato juice while we have our sherry? Phil, darling, help your father." And Phil, who I'd seen blind drunk on straight Scotch during training season, did.

There were candles in the dining-room chandelier, and a woman in a uniform to do the serving. Before we were through the onion soup, Alison had turned into a stranger. We were fairly close friends, tending to sudden eye contact and uncontrollable giggles, but she was aging by the minute, matching Mrs. Lawver's polite and penetrating questions with precise answers. Only her eyes were eager.

"I know nothing about finance, but I should have thought your father got out of banking at just the right moment, Alison. That awful recession hit some people terribly hard."

"Yes," Alison said in a sort of finishing-school voice. "And being in business in Oldfield Village, he can be more active in the community."

"Exactly. We're very pleased to see him ushering at church. You were Episcopalians in New York, before you came up here?"

"I was christened at Trinity."

She'll be asking for a look at Alison's teeth next, I thought. Then I noticed Phil looking at me. I could just see his eye between two chrysanthemums in the bowl on the table. It was like being watched through a hedge. If I'd ever liked being looked at—by anybody—I forgot it immediately. And if I'd ever thought I liked Phil Lawver, I suddenly knew better. I guess I'd always taken him on faith because Alison was so wrapped up in him. Let him look at *her*, I thought and went back to dealing with the onion soup that was turning cold and somewhat slimy.

Mr. Lawver pulled his vest down over his stomach and turned to Steve. "You be going into your family's line of work when you get out of high school, young fellow? You plumbers charge more than doctors."

Then Alison did look at me, quickly, almost apologizing with her eyes. Even Phil stirred.

"Well, Mr. Lawver," Steve said, "I have one older brother who's already in the business with Dad. And another brother who's a lifer in the Marines down at Parris Island. I think I'll strike out in a direction of my own."

"Father," Phil muttered, "Steve here has a perfect academic record. All A's. He's . . . famous for it."

Nobody told *me*." Mr. Lawver cleared his throat. "Well, then, Steve, maybe you and Phil will be going up to Yale together."

"I suppose Steve has a better chance of getting into Yale than I do, Father. If he wants to go."

"You'll get in, Phil." Mr. Lawver patted the tablecloth confidently. "We always get in. Edna, bring in the roast!"

"Hasn't it been curious weather this autumn," Mrs. Lawver remarked. "All that rain and lightning and now so dry."

It seemed a lifetime, but we got away by nine. When Steve and I left, the Lawvers assembled in the front hall, Alison next to Phil. Rehearsing her role, I thought. I didn't envy her. I just marveled at how sure she was about what she wanted. I wasn't sure about anything.

Steve and I didn't say anything until we'd walked the curve of the drive. Then when we passed through the stone gates, we both let out long, relieved sighs. "May the four of them live happily ever after," I said.

"Somehow, I don't think happiness has anything to do with it," Steve said. "What a night. Anyway it was good seeing Edna."

"Edna? Who's Edna?"

"The Lawvers' cook. The silent slave in the uniform. She's my mom's cousin."

"Oh." And that's all I could think of to say to that.

"But back to real life," Steve said as we strolled along in the shadows of the oaks. "If I know my brother's habits, which I do, he'll be down in the Village Center at the Nutmeg Tavern. Let's wander on down there, and I'll borrow his car. Then we can drive out to the lake."

"We'd better not. Mother—"

"I heard your mother when we left. She meant me to. But it's early yet. We'll be back in an hour or so."

We were already walking toward the Village Center instead of back to my house, I noticed. Either Steve was steering me, or my feet had minds of their own. "I don't think we'd better."

"You mean you don't want to."

"Don't push me into that role," I said.

"You mean the well-known playing-hard-to-get?"

"That's the one. It's a little late for that, isn't it?" The leaf shadows made the brick sidewalk wavery underfoot. We paced along with our arms around each other's waist.

"You're still . . ."

"I'm still what?" I said.

"Taking them."

"The pill?"

"Yes. Why not just ask me that all in one sentence?"

"I don't know," he said. "I guess I come from a long line of Italian peasants who don't speak the sacred word s-e-x out loud. But it's more than just that with us, isn't it?"

"I guess—yes. But I don't know how much more. Alison is always—"

"Let's leave Alison out. There's no room for her in this conversation."

"It's just that she's so positive about what she wants. I mean how can she know what'll be right for her ten years from now? I can't see ten minutes ahead." I gave up then because I couldn't get my words to fit around my thoughts. Even talking seemed hopeless, without mentioning basic things like money and what our parents thought and the fact that neither one of us had really gone with other people.

"Just answer me one thing," my mother had said back when Steve and I were first together. "Would you be half as interested in this boy if he weren't the plumber's son? You surely know how clannish these . . . local families can be. What if he were a boy from your own background? Then how would he look to you?"

"Then he wouldn't be Steve," I told her, but she said that was no answer. And it wasn't.

"Some people just concentrate on the present and let the future take care of itself," Steve said finally.

"Are you like that?"

"No."

"Neither am I."

But we went out to the lake anyway. Out to that empty cottage that Steve's dad used for a fishing shack in the summer. The only place where we thought we were alone.

CHAPTER

Two

The next night the eleven o'clock news was winding down through sports and local weather, promising a golden oldie classic for the late show. I sat through the commercials in the faint hope that I hadn't seen the movie before. I had. Victor Mature, Carole Landis, and Betty Grable in *I Wake Up Screaming*. For the second time in a month. And not golden or classic. Just an oldie. The switchboard operator, Harry, kills Carol Landis. And Betty is safe in Victor's arms, but it takes them ninety minutes to get there.

I turned off the set and checked my watch against the mantel clock. Eleven thirty-one. Twenty-nine minutes until the going baby-sitter rate rose seventy-five cents an hour. Not that I was miserly, not then. In fact I felt I owed Mrs. Montgomery a rebate. She always had Angie and Missy fed and bedded before I came on duty, even though the older one was nearly five and hyperactive. So it was easy money at Mrs. Montgomery's. All I had to do was hold the fort and stare at my homework or the set.

She kept a pretty meager refrigerator, but it was always good for a can of Diet-Rite. I drifted down the dark hall to the kitchen. The sink was full of dirty dishes. I wouldn't have minded washing them except that Mrs. Montgomery never exploited her sitters with domestic chores. She didn't go in much for chores herself.

A monument to her heftier days was still taped to the refrigerator door. A curling note lettered in bold black:

A moment on the lips—
Forever on the hips

Right after her divorce she put on a lot of weight. But then she pulled herself together when she joined the Oldfield Village Singles and Previously Marrieds Club. It altered her life, she said. I sat for her every Saturday night, when the club held its parties.

Losing a skirmish with my conscience, I took the last can of Diet-Rite and flipped off the top. I was just walking back through the hall past the phone when it rang. I answered, but no one spoke at the other end.

When I try to remember, now that I know who it was, I wonder if there was any sound. I may have heard breathing, or it may have been my own. Every time I said hello, my voice sounded more and more hollow.

Finally I hung up, and the hellos echoed through the house. I'd just made it back to the living room when the phone rang again. I ran back. But again there was the same tense silence at the other end.

I said hello only once and then felt that tightness in the throat for the first time: the feeling that I was confronting a silent, voiceless, faceless stranger. Somebody reaching out for me.

I stood there in the dimness, pressing the receiver into

my ear. The click came when someone, somewhere, hung up.

The baby sitter's best defense is calm. Whenever I felt a wave of nervousness or even uncertainty, I had the habit of reaching for the small green stone carved in the heart shape. I'd bought a gold chain for it and was never without it. Steve had given it to me for my sixteenth birthday in the spring. I stood there in the hallway with one hand on the receiver and the other working the little stone heart like a worry bead. And then, automatically, I dialed Steve's number.

He answered in the middle of the first ring.

"Home?" he said.

"No. I'm still at Mrs. Montgomery's."

"What's happening?"

"Nothing . . . What are you doing?"

"Reading and listening to a tape."

"What is it?"

"As a matter of fact, it's Rubenstein playing the Chopin Concerto Number One, backed up by the London Symphony, conducted by Skrowaczewski," Steve said like an FM radio announcer.

"Turn it up so I can hear it." I wondered why I'd asked that.

The music welled up in the background. "Have you freaked out over Skrowaczewski?" he said. We went on talking over the Chopin sound. I don't know what we said, but his voice pulled me away from the reason I'd called.

I always liked talking to Steve away from home because I sometimes thought my mother listened on her extension. But I didn't call him every time I baby-sat because of *his* mother. And in Oldfield Village, having a boy over when you're sitting is kind of a taboo. I hadn't broken it yet.

We were running short of conversation when he said, "Gail, you were practically as smooth as Alison last night at Lord and Lady Lawver's. You sound different tonight. You okay?"

"Yes."

"That's good. I miss you." He said that fast. I had a vision of his family sitting in front of the TV one room away, maybe not completely absorbed in *I Wake Up Screaming*. There was a silent moment then, when we both thought of the night before, the rustle from the trees across the lake. The conversation trailed off.

Later I was sitting in the living room, concentrating on the clock. The minute hand was pushing twelve thirty, and I was running the little green heart up and down the gold chain. The warm stone whispered over the tiny links.

Steve had given me my birthday present at school. He'd dropped the little white box on my tray in the cafeteria. I hadn't even noticed it before I lifted the milk carton.

Between the layers of cotton the heart was wrapped in a tube of graph paper, like an ancient scroll. A Steve touch. On the scroll he'd printed a quotation with little flourishes:

> *My heart is turn'd to stone: I strike*
> *it, and it hurts my hand. O, the*
> *world hath not a sweeter creature!*
> *She might lie by an emperor's side,*
> *and command him tasks.*

I cradled it in my palm, Steve's stone heart. And because the clatter of the cafeteria is no place for sentiment, I only said, "I had to fall for an intellectual. I give up. What's the flattering quotation from?"

"You're gaining on me," he said. "Last fall you'd have thought I wrote it myself."

"As a matter of fact, not," I said. "Last fall you were still writing things like, 'I'll weave white violets into—'"

"All right, all right," he said, "forget last fall. It's from *Othello*."

So that night I started reading *Othello*. I tried not to be nudged too far by Steve's attempts at compensatory education. There were times when he made me feel like a benumbed Playboy bunny. And, after all, I was on the honor roll, even if I wasn't on the top of it. I was well into *Othello* before I found out it was about a jealous husband who smothers his wife.

It was like Steve to extract a few lines of love from a tragedy.

Behind the mantel clock was a mirror. Something moved in it and made me shift my gaze from the clock's hands. Somebody had stepped into the dark hall directly behind me. I jumped half off the sofa, and my fingers jerked at the stone heart. The chain popped at the back of my neck and fell in a gold puddle in my hand.

"Oh Lord, Gail, I didn't mean to scare you." Mrs. Montgomery stepped into the light of the living room. Then she turned back into the hall and said to someone out on the front steps, "No, really, I think not. It's late. I'll say good night to you here." As she closed the door, I pulled myself together.

"You must have been miles away not to hear the key in the door," she said, striding into the room. "But look, I'm sorry I scared you. Everything go all right? Kids quiet? Any calls?"

"Calls," I said, "but no one at the other end."

"It's this dratted small town service. The phone's dead half the time and wildly erratic the other half. But they bill you with stunning regularity." She fell into an easy chair and kicked her somewhat knobby feet out of a pair of high-heeled sandals.

"Everybody danced for a good three hours," she said and wiggled her toes. "Just to prove we still can. It was a cross between a college hop and an old folks' home. I wouldn't be your age again for anything, but I wish my feet were." I was already computing my sitter fee. "Well, what's the damage?" When I told her, she said, "I don't worry when you're here. One of the several drawbacks of life in this quaint community is that most of the youngsters—people —your age are so rich they don't need the extra money."

I knew that better than she did. She was digging through her little beaded handbag for the money. When she handed it over, there was a considerable wad. I counted three dollars over.

"It's for the jeweler to fix your chain," she said. And I realized I was still holding it in my hand. I tried to give the money back, but she waved it away. "All my fault," she said.

Then she was struggling back into her shoes and bending over to fasten up the buckles. "I'm driving you home tonight."

"That's silly," I said. "It's only five blocks, and besides the kids—"

"The kids will be all right for ten minutes. You're jumpy and you're pale. You don't need a walk home in the dark, and it's too late to call your dad out of bed to come over for you."

When we were driving along the empty street, Mrs. Montgomery said, "Sometimes I feel guilty tying up your Saturday nights. You go out with the Pastorini boy, don't you?"

"There are absolutely no secrets in this hamlet."

C. 14

"That's where you're wrong," she said with emphasis.

"Yes, we go together. But we sort of . . . limit it."

A loud silence followed. "That's cryptic."

"Well, my parents aren't wild about the idea, and his probably aren't either."

"Romeo and Juliet in western Connecticut," she said. "I can't stand it."

"Neither can I. I get all the selections from Shakespeare I need directly from Steve."

"I must have been misinformed about the youth culture. You go around spouting Shakespeare at each other? I was under the impression you were all majoring in remedial reading—no offense meant."

"Well, Steve's head is packed with scholarship. It occasionally overflows."

"He's very bright, isn't he?"

"Yes."

"And so are you."

"Less intellectual. Maybe less motivated. And we're both very young."

Mrs. Montgomery made a wild turn into our street. "When the very young mention that they're very young, I suspect dark plots and hidden secrets. Do you know what I'm doing?"

"No. What?"

"Idly prying. Tell me to shut up."

"Wouldn't dream of it," I said. "I always profit by talking to older women of broad experience."

"That crack could be the end of a beautiful friendship. End of the line!" she said, taking our front drive too near an ornamental shrub.

The lights of Mrs. Montgomery's car were swinging back down the drive and I was fitting the key into our front door when I heard the ringing inside. But as I ran across the front hall toward the phone, it fell silent.

Yes, I said almost out loud. *I'm home now, whoever you are.*

CHAPTER

Three

A hard frost over the weekend killed Indian summer and turned the sugar maples along Meeting Street into a gold riot. I contemplated rushing winter by putting on my down jacket and my Frye boots, just to limber them up. But settled for digging down to the bottom of the cedar chest for my favorite red English wool scarf. Then I walked out into the postcard-pretty Monday morning, turning the scarf around my neck.

The white spire of the Episcopal church pointed to a dark blue sky. The commuters were gunning along to catch the eight ten to Grand Central. I ambled past the rows of artfully restored houses, breathing in the expensive sub-urban air—past the pale brick center-hall Georgians with their bull's-eye windowpanes, the renovated clapboard inns, the Cape Cod saltboxes, and Mr. Wertheimer's brown-shingled bungalow with the fussy little rock garden in front.

You had to live here for a century or two in order to be-long, but I thought of how we city people outnumbered the locals now: from the Lawvers at one end of the social scale to the Pastorinis somewhat below the middle and right down to the Shulls at the bottom. Our name for the natives was *townies*, but I never used it on Steve.

After a few years and a lot of colonial restoration—a lot of Dutch doors and old glass in new frames and split-shake shingles and carriage lamps beside the doors. And everything in Williamsburg red or Williamsburg green or Williamsburg beige—we tended to look flinty-eyed on new arrivals too. The current wave of people like the Slaneks, who were buying up the barns outside of town to add artiness to the countryside. The townies called them hippiedippies. Slang gets to Oldfield Village late, but it lingers.

I went on past the Lawvers' stone gates. It's the last house before the Village Center. Then came the Bremers' hardware store: The Colonial Craftsman, with a black iron eagle spreading wings over the revolving door. The British Motors Automotive Garage with a cupola on its roof, maybe to help Paul Revere warn the townies that the New Yorkers were coming. Lamston's five and ten, disguised with barn siding. The dinky Pilgrim Theater. And a discreet vine-covered cottage which was the local headquarters of the Planned Parenthood Organization.

I'd paid a visit there last spring, just after my sixteenth birthday. And every time I went past afterward, I walked a little faster. I partly expected Mrs. Raymond to leap out of the front door and scream at me, "Yoo-hoo! I know who *you* are!"

As I turned up Litchfield Street, the sight of our Volvo pulled up at the Sunoco pumps made me stop dead. I knew Mother hadn't taken Dad to the station and then kept the car.

He was standing beside the attendant, watching him fill the tank. He looked like he had all day, and I wondered why he wasn't halfway to work in New York on the seven forty. But I didn't have time to cross over and ask him.

The high school's an exact reproduction of Independence Hall. On the outside. Inside, it's the unadorned, institutional scene, lit by overhead globes filling with dead flies. The halls are lined with banging brown lockers. When I twirled the lock on mine that morning, it reminded me, as usual, of how things had started with Steve.

One day at the very beginning of last year when we'd just moved up from middle school, I found a folded note stuck in the vents on my locker door. I whipped it out and opened it up to find a poem. It was printed with all those little flourishes that later came to stand for Steve in my mind. But not then, of course. It wasn't even signed. It just said:

I'll be so gentle you won't know I'm there
I'll weave white violets into your hair
For there isn't anything I wouldn't share
And one day you'll know just how much I can care.

I didn't know what to make of it. This off-season valentine. This home-grown Hallmark card. Being fifteen and starved for romance, I was pretty curious to know who'd sent it. But then I decided it was really meant for Alison. She and I always had adjoining lockers, and the boys had always buzzed around her even before they were buzzing around anybody: before she settled in with Phil Lawver.

But hope and pride mingled to keep me from readdressing the note to Alison's locker vents. Then, a couple of weeks later when I'd half forgotten about it, I found some ugly little white plastic flowers stuck in the vents. Lamston products and not quite violet-shaped, but I made the connection.

I'd felt eyes boring into my back. And I turned around to find Steve Pastorini behind me, trying to look casual. I won't say I hadn't noticed him before. I had. Curly dark hair, glasses repaired with tape at the nosepiece, and one of those rock-hard chins more New England than Italian, softened by the eyes. He was a townie, or I'd have already known him better. And he had a reputation as a bustass, which is our vulgar term for an overachiever, academically. It was later that I found out he studied most of his waking hours because he wanted to, not because he had to.

He was leaning against the opposite row of lockers with the heels of his construction boots together and his hands jammed down in his Levi pockets. We walked out of school together that afternoon.

What was it like at first? We talked in riddles and circled around each other with probing words. "What's your very favorite . . .?" "What's the first thing you can remember?" "What would you do if you didn't have to do anything?" And, "Why aren't you more like me?" "Why aren't I more like you?" Finally, "Did you ever like-love anybody before? This much?"

All the questions everyone asks without leaving time enough for answers. Wanting to close all the distances between us fast to make up for all those thousands of years we hadn't known each other. We were on opposite sides of the ethnic fence, and then we were holding each other very close. Like every other two people drawing together, we were brother and sister, and then we were lovers. And after that we weren't sure what we were.

It didn't take the other kids long to think of us as kind of an old married couple. The cooler you act, the quicker they know.

I'd only met his family once. It was back early last spring, and we'd walked all the way out to his house after school, meaning to do homework together. I figured out early that with Steve learning had a higher priority than loving. We were still pretty much in the hand-holding stage. Later, I guess he wouldn't have taken me home.

The Pastorinis lived in a house with a big front porch across the front, the badge of a townie family. The first thing New Yorkers do is tear off the porch and replace it with dwarf evergreens. And it was painted blue. Not Williamsburg blue. Robin's-egg blue.

The Pastorinis had a big country kitchen with a deep freeze the size of a coffin and there was oilcloth on the table. A linoleum square was laid like a rug on the floor, not quite reaching to the walls. There was a fluorescent fixture in the ceiling and a picture of Jesus, with dried palms from Palm Sunday tacked behind, on one of the cupboard doors. I pretended it didn't seem strange, but I looked around a lot.

Mrs. Pastorini didn't seem to want to come into the kitchen. But it was getting on toward dinner time ("supper time" at their house), and finally she hurried in to the stove. "You kids just keep right on with your work," she said, smiling shyly.

I was trying to do a theme for English and got, I think, about four or five sentences written. Steve's dad came home and was in the middle of the kitchen before he saw us there. He couldn't place me, not even after Steve mumbled a kind of introduction.

The thing I noticed about Steve's parents can't be put into words. They didn't say that much. They were gentle, gentler than he was in a way. But there was a definite feeling in that kitchen. They were respectful toward him. That's the only word I can think of. His dad was a great big man, with hands the size of baseball mitts—nothing like Steve's hands at all. "I used to try and help him when he took math," Mr. Pastorini said to me. Even if he couldn't figure out who I was, he was pleased that I seemed to be studying. "Oh, I guess that was back about the eighth grade. Seems like last night, but it wasn't. When he come to algebra, though, he was away over my head. Didn't need any help off of me anyhow."

"Oh, come on, Dad," Steve said. But Mr. Pastorini just stood over us, beaming down at him.

Alison rushed up to her locker. We had six more jumps on the hall clock before the bell for drama class. Describing first love is a little like describing the person you once thought was your best friend. It's safer to stick to surface impressions—the way the firelight from the Lawvers' hearth had played across her serene-looking face that Friday night. She had a highly polished surface.

I remember two or three summers ago she'd said to a girl we both knew, "You must be getting popular. I see you everywhere I go." She'd refined her approach since then. More human, I thought. But whether she was getting more human or less, I always remembered how much I liked her when I first came to Connecticut.

I was in the I-hate-everything eleven-year-old stage anyway, and moving out of New York to the boondocks was a bitter pill. Was I glad that practically the first person who even looked my way at school was Alison Bremer. She hardly even remembered living in New York herself. Still, she put up with my instant nostalgia for the Big Town. And in my books that made her *neat*, my all-purpose word of approval. Once when my mother still went back to shop in Manhattan, she took Alison and me along. There wasn't much shopping. Instead we went to see the Rockettes' morning show and then had lunch at the Soup Bar at Lord & Taylor. We wore ourselves out that day, and I realized I was glad to come home to Oldfield Village. I don't suppose Alison even remembered that time. She kept her sights pretty much on the future.

I could see her future myself. Even without the Lawver connection, she projected a clear image of an uppercrust Oldfield Village society dame. I could see her spending the rest of her life slipping in and out of a wood-paneled station wagon in a gored skirt with a Gucci bag on her arm. Never more than just pretty enough. And always in her usual kind of easy-going haste. She'd go to Yale or to its nearest women's college and then come back to marry Phil and be the queen of the PTA.

"Good thing we've got drama first period," she said, throwing and grabbing at her books. "I can get the geometry finished. Did you get it?"

"All but the last three problems."

"Shoot. Those are the ones I don't have."

And then Alison and I observed a moment of silence. Sonia Slanek was coming to school. That was her first year there—her only year. So we'd had just six weeks to study her. The Slaneks lived in a converted barn out on the Woodbury Road. Her father was a sculptor, with his studio in the haymow. People said they'd come from the SoHo district of New York where artists have their lofts. I think as far as Sonia was concerned, she was still back there.

She lived in her own private world, and you could read that much in her eyes, which were fixed and just slightly out of focus. None of us had ever seen anything like her. It was as if she dedicated her whole life to creating a work of very weird modern art—bizarre and beautiful in a way. And the art object was herself.

Her hair was auburn—about the color of mine. But every day it was different, rolled sometimes in a flattened mushroom shape or pompadoured like the 1940s.

Without the makeup, her face might have been relatively blah. It was heart-shaped, and the cleft in her chin was its only landmark without the cosmetics. On that Monday morning her eyelids were wonderfully shaded in pale peacock blue. Penciled in just beyond the ends of her plucked eyebrows were the suggestions of butterfly wings. Her mouth was very small, and she'd reshaped it in subtle brown lipstick with little Cupid's-bow points at the center of her upper lip.

She was wearing a black monkey-fur jacket with three-quarter sleeves. It was obviously a Women's Exchange rummage sale item. But burnished, even combed, to perfection. It had never looked that good on the monkey. She wore long black kid gloves, the kind grand matrons wear in old movies. And on one wrist, over the glove, a single, perfectly plain ivory bracelet.

Her slacks were velvet printed in art deco pyramids and rainbows, all colors, and enormously belled at the bottom. The cuffs swished around a pair of lemon yellow shoes with three-inch platforms. She walked directly down the center of the hall, swaying slightly. I don't suppose she even had a locker. She never carried books. Whenever she took notes in a class, she drew out a small stenographic pad from her needlepoint purse and wrote in it with a pen that had a long tassel on it.

"It's kitsch," Alison said, "but she's certainly got it all together."

The bell rang then, and we darted off to meet the second extreme character of the day.

After Sonia, if there's such a thing as a bright spot in a school day, it was the class presided over by a woman named Dovima Malevich. Most of the seniors and as many of us juniors as could get in rioted to take her class. She was perfectly capable of saying, "Call me Madam," and she said she was Russian. Her accent came and went. But there were no other Russians around Oldfield Village to challenge her claim.

She had a hawk's head perched on a pigeon's body. Her hair seemed to be painted on in black lacquer with a wide white center part. Even adults regarded her as elderly. She had to be well past seventy-five, they said. The only reason she had the teaching job was that she'd been a friend of the late senior Mrs. Lawver, who'd run the school board like Catherine the Great.

The senior Mrs. Lawver was in the ground, but Madam Malevich taught on, in defiance of the Connecticut retirement laws. "I haf bin in for small talk wiz the principal," she'd sometimes say at the beginning of class when her accent was heaviest. "And we haf come to another of our unnerstandings."

This meant that the principal had again invited her to retire, and she'd again declined the invitation. To us, the principal was a myth because he never came out of his office. To Madam Malevich he was a joke. He was young enough to be her son, but I suppose she just planned to outlive him. Maybe she will.

Drama was an elective. Still, we turned our schedules inside out to get in her class. It was known as an easy A when Madam Malevich bothered to record the grades. But more than that, she seemed to fill a hole in our neat, set lives. She didn't teach drama as a subject. She *was* the drama, and to her the world really was a stage.

She'd never been known to mount a student production. "I haf no time for amateurs. Young persons truly innerested in a theatrical career do not piddle their time away in Oldfield Village," she said more than once. "If they are at school at all, they are attending the High School for Performing Arts in New York City and going for auditions and open calls in their free time.

"And what are *you* doing in your bounteous free time?" she would ask, scanning the class with a cobra's eye. "Malevich will tell you! Making puppy's eyes at one another at Shakey's Pitzah Parlor and Friendly's Ice Cream Store and volfing Big Macs in parking lots and making the road to Powdermill Lake perilous wiz your fresh new drivers' licenses!"

This stinging attack on our life style brought forth satisfied grins from all over the room. What other teacher even recognized that we had a life style?

"Or you, Barnie Whitman," she said that Monday morning, warming up. "Your free time is gobbled up tuning that Pinto car of yours." She pointed an arthritic, bright-nailed finger at his slouching form. Barnie, a townie, ducked his head and smiled proudly at his grease-blackened paws.

"My God, is a piece of junk of the Ford Motor Company a fine Stradivarius violin to be tuned wiz such delicacy?"

Her eye swept over Sonia, but she never put her on the spot. Of course, she couldn't miss her. Maybe Sonia's stage makeup and monkey fur reminded Madam Malevich of an earlier, more glamourous age. Or maybe Sonia was a relief from the safe sameness of the rest of us. Later I thought about that and wonder still.

"Alison Bremer, is that geometry you do in your lap? Put it avay. Mathematics? No. If you haf talents, they lie elsewhere." And then her eyes rose halfway up her forehead, and they seemed to embrace the whole room, waiting with professional timing for our reaction. Giggles, more grins, and even applause because we knew this was a performance: Malevich without malice.

We knew, too, that, crackpot though she was, she observed us with a sharp eye, in between bouts of vagueness. Most of the kids thought she was actually crazy, but I never did.

And always before her monologue rambled on to the theater or film-making, she'd hit us with the one-liner to bring us down in a heap: "My God, all so young and so lifeless. At your age already I vas *somebody*!"

CHAPTER

Four

"Yes, but who?" Steve said at lunch. "You're always reporting that she was somebody, but who?"

"How do I know?" I said. "She doesn't dwell on the past like most old people do. I suppose she was an actress or something."

"Are you interested in drama, and does she teach any?"

"Not much—to both questions."

"Then why waste your time on that joke course?" Steve was in one of his dark, Lord Byron moods, and I was wishing lunch was over because there was no talking him out of them. He took Advanced Placement History while I was being entertained by Madam Malevich. And he was always getting at me about not being bustass enough.

"I doubt that I qualify for AP History, for one thing," I said, skidding deeper into the argument. "And anyway, 'History is little else than a picture of human crimes and misfortunes.' "

"Where did you dig up Voltaire to throw at me?" he asked, half interested.

"Bartlett's *Familiar Quotations*. I got ready for this argument because we've had it before. Does it strike you that we're fighting more lately and making up less?"

"Not particularly."

We'd finished eating, and so there was nothing left to do with our hands. I gazed at his. They weren't a boy's hands. They were long and tapering and strong. When we argued, I always escaped by thinking of those man's hands cradling my face, caressing the back of my neck, touching my hair. Weaving imaginary white violets in it, I guess.

"Maybe you have too much drive, and I don't have enough. Maybe we're just not suited to each other." It sounded weirdly like my mother practicing ventriloquism with me as the dummy.

Why couldn't we just let each other go? It was a first love, and it was cooling. There'd be others, for both of us. I can say that now, I couldn't then. I'd have bitten off my tongue first.

"Maybe you're looking for excuses to break up. Keep looking and you'll find them," Steve said in a low, acidy voice.

"I'm not looking for anything," I said, which meant nothing. I was still staring at his hands, but I could feel his brown eyes behind the glasses trained on my face.

"It's just that I hate seeing you fall in with Alison and the rest of them," he said.

"But I *am* one of the rest of them. I'm just another decadent New Yorker who pushed in here and ruined the town for its rightful owners. And as far as Alison's concerned, she's my best friend, and believe me I could use one!"

"I'm glad to hear it," Alison said, suddenly appearing, tray in hand. "I don't want to butt in, but this sounds like a conversation that could have a sticky end."

"A slick line, Alison," Steve said. "And true. Sit down. I have to go to the chem lab before fifth period. You can have my chair. In fact, you're welcome to it."

"What's he going to do in the chem lab in that mood—blow himself up?" Alison murmured to me. She was determined to lighten the mood. As Steve turned away, making a point of not saying anything to me, she said, "Oh Steve, are you coming to the squash match? It'll be Phil's moment of glory. He's planning to murder Exeter."

First Madam Malevich and now a squash match. In Steve's view there was no end to our frivolities. "No. I've got to help Dad after school and then get in a couple of hours at the library before it closes."

When he was gone, Alison said, "He's really bearing down on that I'm-from-a-working-class-family-and-don't-you-forget-it bit, isn't he? You're in for a bumpy road with that guy. He's sexy, though."

"What do you know about it?" I said, and we were off, giggling those giggles Steve loathed.

But then, very soberly, Alison said, "Phil's such a . . . New England puritan. I fantasize about other guys sometimes."

On the squash court Phil Lawver was aggressive enough. He wore a leather support glove on his serving hand, and even his practice shots slammed the small black ball in blurring zigzags that hit every wall.

The school has squash mainly to give it tone. We competed with the private schools where it's very big. A gentleman's game. And that day we were playing the top two players from Exeter Academy, where they have thirteen courts and the game's nearly a religion.

Phil's teammate was another superior townie, Buddy

McEvoy. He was short, wiry, and, I thought, creepy. He held the racket lightly in his spidery hand and wore a sweatband. Phil and he were well-practiced partners, bobbing and weaving and never falling over each other. Phil —tall and tense. Buddy—low-slung and loose.

The Exeter boys, still in their warm-up suits, kept giving them worried looks out of the corners of their eyes. The game was slow in starting. Though the referees were already in their positions around the balcony, Coach Foster was still on the court, fiddling with towels and trying to give Phil and Buddy unnecessary last-minute pointers. He was the kind of coach who always wears shorts: a middle-aged adolescent.

Finally it got going, and Oldfield won the serve. Phil, the golden boy, drew his racket back in slow motion, and the ball seemed to explode against the far wall, just above the line. The cube we sat in was deafening with the sound of the ball and the skid of shoes on the floor. My mind wandered. I was there only because of Alison, and her eyes never left Phil.

But he was in another world of frenzied, punishing action. I never have understood the jock mentality. He'd ricochet against the side wall sometimes, knocking the wind out of himself. But only for a split second. Then he'd be back in position, and you could see his grip tightening on the racket. He was all over the court, working Exeter harder and harder.

We took them, three out of five. The coach was on the floor before the first spatter of applause, trying to toss towels over all the players' necks. Phil twirled his racket on the court and wrenched off the glove. When Buddy McEvoy ran over to throw his arms around him, Phil dodged past to shake the hands of the Exeter players. They looked dazed by the trouncing. But they took the diplomat's hand. There was a look of well-bred disgust on their faces for coming all the way from New Hampshire to get wiped out by a public school.

Alison sat forward on the bleacher seat, wishing for Phil to look up at her, but he was holding the locker-room door for the other team. Suddenly the court was empty and quiet. After the stands cleared, we strolled out onto the campus, and Alison lit up a Virginia Slim. She cradled one hand under her elbow and blew smoke up into the tree limbs.

She was only half through it when she flipped it away and said, "I'm not going to wait for Phil. He's foul company after a match. Takes him all evening to unwind."

That wasn't what she meant at all. Alison and I could often read each other's mind. "Who am I trying to kid?" she said. "Phil's probably dressed and already gone. I could stand under this tree all night, undiscovered. It's funny about him. He keeps me in one of two places. Half the time I'm on a pedestal. The other half, I'm in a closet. Sometimes I wonder why I bother."

But we both knew why Alison bothered. All that status and security Phil and his family stood for. And without another word we headed back into school. When we got to our lockers, it was nearly five. The janitors were beginning to push their brooms down the hall. I suppose Alison and I both saw it at the same time. There was a note sticking out of the vent in my locker.

It was painstakingly folded into the smallest possible shape. I pulled it out, and in block letters on the outside was my full name. GAIL OSBURNE.

Let there be no mistake about who this note is for, I thought even before I unfolded it. Somehow, I didn't want to open it at all. Alison was just behind me, not even pretending to turn her lock.

Inside the neat lettering was black on the page right down to the bottom. Someone had a lot to say. The first line began, "I'M WATCHING YOU, YOU—"

That's almost the only line I can make myself repeat now. My mind kept rejecting the words. Instead I noticed the even margins, the accurate punctuation. But the words. All the things someone thought I was. And all the things someone planned to do to me, to make me do. Every perverted, sadistic, sick, and sickening ugly act. A twisted porno movie playing in somebody's brain.

And then at the bottom, in block letters, centered perfectly:

YOU KNOW YOU WANT IT. YOU'LL GET IT. AND YOU WON'T HAVE LONG TO WAIT.

I held onto the page because my hands were frozen. I could hear Alison's breathing beside my ear, coming in shorter and shorter gasps. I could even hear the bump and slide of the janitors' brooms. And my heart.

"Stop it!" Alison shrieked. "Stop reading that garbage!" She reached around me and grabbed the paper out of my hand. I think I was grateful. I didn't want it to be there. "It isn't—"

"It isn't what?" I needed to keep hearing a human voice.

"I don't know what I mean. It isn't anybody we know. It couldn't be."

"I think it is," I said. "But it isn't anybody sane." Then I started running.

The white picket fences flashed by. And I pounded on over the sidewalks past the solid old trees whose roots made mounds and breaks in the bricks. I was sure if I looked up,

I'd see some terrible crack running across the perfect blue dome of the sky. And maybe the spire of the Episcopal church lying on its side.

At the first sight of our house, I had to stop running. I'd outgrown the kid's privilege of dashing home—with a skinned knee or something—and bursting into tears at the front door.

But when I got there, my eyes and my face and my throat were dry. I felt sick, but the running had helped that too. When I pushed open the front door, I noticed for the first time that unless we were all away, we never kept it locked.

Inside, I tried to let the house calm me. The antique ivory wall paneling that followed the staircase up and curved with it at the landing. The little pewter candlestick lamp on the stand beside the telephone. All orderly, ordinary, usual.

I thought the house was empty, and that seemed right because I'd never felt so alone. But my mother was sitting in the living room. The lights weren't on, and she was sitting in the leather chair holding a drink. Neither the darkness nor the drink seemed odd at the time.

"Gail, come in here." It was pointless to try to act like nothing was wrong, but I tried. It'd been a long time since I'd felt like confiding in my mother.

"Look at you," she said, putting down her drink. "You're trying not to cry. What has that Steve Pastorini done to you?"

CHAPTER

Five

The tears burned my eyes and probably gleamed in the dark. I'd heard my mother's one-liners on Steve a hundred times. Now of all times I had to hear the same thing again. It was like being pushed very near the edge of some place deep, possibly bottomless.

She was sitting there in the trim tweed pants outfit she often changed into just before Dad came home. I'd always tried to match her pulled-together coolness, and it was a game neither of us won. Maybe she didn't seem as . . . untouchable to me as she once had, but we still weren't getting through to each other.

"Sit down. Something's wrong, and if it isn't Steve, who is it?"

"I don't know." That much was true, but of course it didn't sound true. It sounded like I was covering up for Steve. The crazy thought flashed through my mind that I was. But then I wasn't in control of my thoughts. Except to know that I couldn't tell my mother about that note. I could feel the filth of it smeared on me. And nobody was going to see that, especially her. Nothing like that could ever possibly have happened to her. What I really wanted was a long, steaming hot bath.

But I wasn't going to get it. She'd have followed me up the stairs.

"I don't have anything against Steve—or his family whom we don't even know. But I don't see the point in your getting emotionally involved when you so obviously aren't right for each other."

"But then you don't know him very well, do you, Mother?" I was falling right in with her, trying to match that mildly bored, all-knowing New York tone.

"How could I? When he comes to pick you up for a date, he hardly crosses the threshold."

"He's not a clod, Mother. He's sensitive enough to know where he's not welcome." Challenging my mother's hospitality was a cheap shot, and I knew it. The whole point in living in Oldfield Village was to play the social game by the rules. I couldn't go on with this argument even though it was an escape from what was really on my mind.

"Look, Mother, Steve isn't the problem right now, as far as I'm concerned. Please, let's just leave it at that."

"Gail, have you and Steve— I mean, are you and he—"

"Mother, please don't ask me that."

The Volvo honked in the drive: Dad announcing himself. Mother jumped out of her chair and flicked on one of the lamps. She remembered the glass on the table. And in the confidential voice she uses with her friends, she said, "I just felt I had to have a drink this evening for some reason." She looked right at me, and there wasn't any coolness in her eyes.

She picked up the drink and almost ran out to the

kitchen with it. I heard the ice cubes clinking into the sink just before Dad opened the back door. We didn't lock that either.

It was the middle of that week when Mother started a night-school course at Danbury. She didn't say anything about it until the last minute. I'd supposed she was probably going to take lessons in flower arranging or gourmet cooking, but it was a class in how to sell real estate. She saw I was surprised at that, but it was time for her to leave. She was dropping Dad at a board meeting. He sat on a community planning committee, approving architectural restoration proposals.

As they left, Mother delivered her usual speech. "You won't have any of your friends over while we're gone, will you, Gail?"

"No, Mother, I won't ask Steve over."

Having the house to myself had always been a luxury. But the minute I was alone, the note seemed to materialize in my hands.

I'M WATCHING YOU, YOU . . .

If I'd only been able to talk it over with someone.

YOU KNOW YOU WANT IT . . .

And Alison knew. But we hadn't mentioned it. We'd been careful not to. I couldn't bring it up, and, I supposed, neither could she. Maybe she could understand how dirty it made me feel. I'd left the note in her hands.

But we were the only two who knew. No, that wasn't right.

YOU'LL GET IT . . .

We were two out of the three who knew. I never considered telling Steve about it.

AND YOU WON'T HAVE LONG TO WAIT . . .

I was up in my room later, just standing around, when the phone rang. It must have been ringing in my head before it even started. It went on and on while I stood with one hand flat and damp against the cool glass top on my dressing table. Then I knew the ringing would never stop until I answered, no matter how long I waited. Someone knew I was in the house by myself. Someone knew where I was all the time.

I went in to Mother and Dad's room where the extension is and sat down on their bed. There was only the light from the hall slanting in across the bedspread and my hands bunched in my lap.

When I picked up the receiver, I didn't say anything. The voice at the other end said just one word. I knew what it was and what it meant. You see it written on walls sometimes.

He said it so fast that it could have been anybody's voice. Then the click. Then the dial tone.

There are twenty-eight windows in our house. I know because I checked the lock on every one of them. I'd turn off the lights at the doors before I went into the rooms. I knew how I'd look, silhouetted against the glow of one window after another. It was as if I could almost be the stranger who might be standing under the trees at the end of the lawn. The stranger who maybe followed me around all four sides of the house, moving from shadow to shadow. Except that he wasn't a stranger.

Each time I checked a window upstairs, I imagined I heard a ladder against the side of the house. Downstairs,

I'd stand in a dark room, keeping clear of a window, before I went over to it. The shapes of the evergreens outside began to look like human forms. I'd stand against the opposite wall, waiting for them to turn back into trees. But they took their time about it.

I wasn't quite in my right mind, or I wouldn't have checked all the windows before remembering the doors. When I did, I ran at all of them, turning both the lock and bolt knobs.

From the kitchen window I saw the garage door was pushed up. Anybody—anybody at all—could see the car was gone. Finally I went to bed. It was easier than standing in the dark, waiting.

I lay up there for two hours, wondering where all the security of nestling into a familiar bed had gone. Wondering what I'd spent all my life thinking about before those past few days. Wondering if it was only the wind or the rustle of footsteps in the leaves on the lawn. Wondering what I should do.

I didn't sleep, and so I heard our car drive in and the garage door rumble down. Dad had to use two keys on the back door, and I heard them both turn in the locks. Then Mother opened my door and said, "For heaven's sake, Gail, why did you leave the phone off the hook? It's absolutely squawking."

But my eyes were closed and my breathing was regular and my mouth was slightly open. I seemed to be asleep.

At school I was closer to him, whoever he was. At our lockers the next morning, I said to Alison, "I wish we could talk about it. The note."

She looked at me around her locker door. I could only see half of her face. "It never happened, Gail."

"Is that the way to handle it?" She bewildered me.

"Yes," she said, and walked away, not even waiting for me or for the arrival of Sonia Slanek.

When Sonia did appear, coming down the middle of the hall with the crowd dividing to make way for her, I envied the sealed-off world she lived in. Even the befurred, be-jeweled, painted shell she put between herself and the rest of us.

All that day I didn't know what I dreaded more. The next message, or Saturday night, baby-sitting at Mrs. Montgomery's. It never occurred to me to quit the job. I already felt alone wherever I was.

After Mrs. Montgomery left, I went up and looked in on the kids. One was asleep in a baby bed, the other in a junior bed with her arms thrown back and little bubbles on her lips. Scattered around on the floor were big stuffed Snoopies and a Cookie Monster hand puppet and a Star Trek coloring book. I stepped quietly around them to check the locks on the windows. Lights blazed from the house next door, and I tried to remember the name of the neighbors.

Downstairs the living-room curtains were all drawn. I glanced into the dining room, but there were gauzy white tie-backs on those windows and blackness beyond. So I stayed in the living room, staring at the television for an age before realizing I'd turned the sound too low to hear. I guess I didn't want to miss hearing the phone.

It rang then. And I let it. Thirty times after I started counting. A long fifteen minutes later it started again and wouldn't stop. *I've already heard all the words. What does it matter?* I lifted the receiver and heard music in the background.

When I didn't say hello, Mrs. Montgomery said, "Gail, my heavens, are you all right? Surely you heard the phone!

I'm sitting in this booth in an absolute panic. What's wrong?"

I owed her an explanation. My mind searched for excuses instead. "The television, it was blaring."

"Are you sure you're all right? I thought I'd just call to check, and then when—"

"Everything's fine and the kids are sound asleep. Are you having a good time?" I could hear the Previously Marrieds dance band in the background playing "That Old Black Magic."

"I'm having the usual time," Mrs. Montgomery said. "Actually my feet are killing me, and I'm sitting this set out. Anyway, Bob Foster has dumped me and gone off to the card room to play poker, or somewhere. It's not one of our cozier nights."

"Who's Bob Foster?"

"You have to ask? He's the coach at the high school."

"Coach Foster? You mean that you and he—"

"I told you this town still had some secrets. Who do you think I dance with at this club—Tony Orlando?" I'd thought I'd convinced her nothing was wrong at my end, but she mentioned that she'd be home early, before midnight. After she hung up, I forgot to ask if she'd tried to call before. Maybe I didn't want to know.

She was home in half an hour. I heard her voice and Coach Foster's all the way up the front walk. Opening the front door, I tried to look responsible. Mrs. Montgomery had that look on her face that nice people get when they're concerned about you. "Gail, you know Coach Foster, don't you?"

The coach loomed over her shoulder. I'd never seen him in long pants before, let alone a suit and clip-on bow tie. He grunted something at this introduction.

"We haven't exactly met before," I said. "They haven't let a girls' team on the squash court yet."

Coach Foster grunted again at that. He looked sickened at the idea of girls on his squash court. I think he was the only man I'd ever seen who still had crew-cut hair. It was sparse and gray.

They came into the hall, and Mrs. Montgomery said, "Oh, Bob, go on out to the kitchen. In the pantry there's a bottle of White Label with a couple of fingers of Scotch left in it. Fix one for me with a splash of soda. And there's Gatorade in the refrigerator for you."

When he lumbered off, she led me straight into the living room. She made a long business of digging my money out of her evening bag. I sat there facing her and feeling guilty about not answering the phone. It seemed I was beginning to feel guilty about a lot of things that weren't my fault.

"If there's anything that's worrying you, Gail," she said, not looking up from her open purse, "anything at all, you can tell me. After all, as long as you're sitting with the kids, your problems are mine. If you have any, I mean. You know, we single ladies have to stick together." She looked up and smiled, a little too brightly.

Whatever I might have said was cut off by Coach Foster, who came into the living room drinking his Gatorade from the bottle. When he handed Mrs. Montgomery her drink, he shot me an irritated look. He wasn't happy to find me still there.

He was less happy when she said, "Oh, Bob, you wouldn't mind driving Gail home, would you." He started to say something, but she didn't let him. "You can come back afterwards and . . . ah . . . finish your Gatorade."

It was a moonless, inky-black night. When we drove off

into it, I fought the urge to plaster myself up against the car door. Keeping my distance from Coach Foster. He didn't help matters by driving along in silence. With any other teacher, I'd have thought I should make some conversation. But then I didn't think of him as a teacher. He was more like a sulky kid. A very big one.

Something was gnawing at me. Something Mrs. Montgomery had said on the phone about how the coach had wandered off somewhere during the dance. He could have slipped into a phone booth and . . . and I had to stop thinking things like that.

All I wanted was to get home. Then I saw we were almost there, and he'd made all the right turns without asking me where I lived. It was a small thing, but it panicked me. He knew where I lived. Lots of people did, of course. But that was the problem.

When he pulled into our drive, I jerked at the door handle. "Not so fast!" I froze. "Don't open a door till a car comes to a stop." He growled that out in his squash-court voice. But the car was stopped by then, and in the next second I was swinging my feet out. Somehow, though, I knew he was reaching across toward me. I whirled around to see his big paw bang the door shut and push the lock button down.

"Thanks," I yelled, too late. "Thanks for the ride!" He nodded, I think, and the car backed down the drive. It swung around and peeled off in the direction of Mrs. Montgomery's house.

Instead of running for the front door, I stood beside the drive, watching the car out of sight. I just kept standing there in the middle of the night, tempting fate. Wanting something to happen and then be over. I knew I couldn't go on much longer being afraid of everybody.

There was a word for that. A psychiatric kind of word. I could end up in a room with bolts on the door and bars on the window and no phone. I was beginning to yearn for that room. And maybe, I thought, maybe that yearning was what I really had to fear.

It was the middle of the next week when I got the second note. And it was the last one.

CHAPTER

Six

You'd think broad daylight and a school full of kids would be better than sitting alone in a house at night. But it wasn't. I guess I began to lose some of my perceptions and sharpen others. I was always looking over my shoulder, but I couldn't concentrate on the regular routine.

Miss Gernreich held me up to public ridicule in geometry when I couldn't do last night's easiest problem on the board. Then later, when she took my homework out of my hand and found I'd done every problem practically right, she gave me a strange look.

But boys. Men. I was looking at them all the time. Trying to see into them. Which was the rotten one? Or were they all rotten? If I didn't know which one to fear, how could I keep from fearing them all? And hating them? And where did that get me?

I stood at the drinking fountain so long that I was late for English just because I noticed Buddy McEvoy hanging around with his usual gang. I strained to hear what they were talking about. I couldn't take my eyes off his spidery hand holding a notebook the way he held a squash racket.

Then I dropped him and thought about all the guys I didn't even know. There was a whole subculture of townie creeps with boots and Hondas and no place to go. We called them sweathogs. And I was just snobbish enough not even to know their names.

English was taught by the meekest, mildest man on the faculty, Mr. Bauman. He always wore a black tie, and even when he was around, you thought you were in the room alone. And now that was the very thing that worried me about him. How could I know what his frustrations were? And when I tried to imagine them, I couldn't think about anything else.

We were doing nineteenth-century English poetry from purple mimeographed sheets. Mr. Bauman always came out of himself a little when he read poetry aloud. The poem for that day was Wordsworth's "Strange Fits of Passion I Have Known." I guess I went a little batty during the second stanza.

> *When she I loved looked every day*
> *Fresh as a rose in June,*
> *I to her cottage bent my way,*
> *Beneath an evening-moon.*

I knew it was a regular love poem of the soulful kind. We'd done them before. But in those four lines I could only see someone creeping toward a girl alone in a big old house, out on the moors, someone getting closer and closer as he bent his way. *Be careful*, I said to the girl in the poem. *Bar the door. Protect yourself. Get help.*

Mr. Bauman had stopped reciting. Everybody in the room had turned to look at me, everybody but Alison.

Whatever I'd just thought, I'd said out loud. I looked down, pretending to read the poem, but it was all crumpled up in my hand and the purple ink looked like webs.

"Gail Osburne?" Mr. Bauman said in his soft voice. "Do you have a comment to contribute?"

I shook my head fast and never looked up. Mr. Bauman's voice droned on through the poem.

> *My horse moved on; hoof after hoof*
> *He raised, and never stopped:*
> *When down behind the cottage roof,*
> *At once, the bright moon dropped.*

But he got all the way to the end of the poem before people stopped giving me sidelong glances.

> *What fond and wayward thoughts will slide*
> *Into a Lover's head!*
> *"Oh, mercy!" to myself I cried,*
> *"If Lucy should be dead."*

Finally the day was over. And four more to go. While I was fumbling with my combination lock, somebody stepped up behind me and grabbed me by the shoulders. I jumped, banged my head on the door. Books spilled out of my arms and all over the floor. "Oh *please, please* leave me alone!" I turned to see Steve standing there.

"What is it?" he said. And when I looked in his eyes, I could tell that somebody had told him I'd been acting strange in English class, of all places. "What's the problem?"

I started to tell him—everything. But Alison came up then, looking around at my books all over the floor. And while I couldn't think why, I didn't want her to hear me telling Steve. Either that or I didn't want her to hear what he'd reply.

Worried? Embarrassed? Scared? I couldn't sort through everything I was feeling.

"Look," Steve said, frowning at me, trying to analyze me. "What about doing something after school tomorrow?" Tomorrow? Tomorrow would be a repeat of today, I knew. Unless I did something about it.

"Tomorrow will be fine," I told him.

The next morning, when everybody else was filing into Madam Malevich's class, I was on the train to New York. I had enough baby-sitting money saved to get halfway to Florida, and that's just where I wished I was going. But I was on the late commuters' train for Grand Central. My dad had left the house at his usual time, and I figured I'd catch him at his office before he got too involved with his day.

I'd spent an evening pretending that it was all over. No more calls or notes. And it hadn't worked. It was time to tell somebody. Alison hadn't been any help at all. Where are people when you need them?

What I expected Dad to do, I don't know now. Call the police? Keep me home? Watch me night and day? I was already being watched night and day. I knew how that felt. And why did I think that cutting school to see Dad would keep Mother from knowing? I just wasn't thinking. I was running.

It was a new experience—the train at rush hour. When I looked around, I saw I was the only female in the car. It was packed with Oldfield Village businessmen in trench coats and Brooks Brothers suits. All the faces were smooth as eggs, bent to folded copies of the *Wall Street Journal*. My faceless, unknowable neighbors.

I barely knew or remembered New York well enough to find the right subway train to Dad's office. The local roared in before the express or I'd have gone hopelessly astray.

Lichtner, Purdy, & Osburne, A.I.A., was housed in a little barn-shaped building amid the high rises. By the time I got to the door, it was eleven thirty and I was at large in the middle of Manhattan. If I collapsed dead on the sidewalk, a thousand people would step neatly over me and keep moving. But I felt a thousand times safer there than in Oldfield Village.

The reception room was empty, but I didn't have the nerve to walk past the receptionist's desk. In a moment she came out of a cubbyhole with a mug of tea in her hand. She was the real New York item. Wild black hair in a halo of ringlets. Steel-rimmed glasses on a face that had seen twenty-five years of disillusionment, starting at birth.

"Oh hi," she said, "been waiting long?" Her tongue searched around in her cheek, found a wad of gum, and she began to chew. "Like you want to see somebody?"

I cleared my throat, decided this had all been a wrong idea. "Mr. Osburne."

"Who? Mr. Osburne? You're about a month late. Mr. Osburne isn't with us any more. You want to see somebody else?"

"I mean Mr. Neal Osburne. He's a partner in the firm."

"Not any more," she said. "Say listen, are you like . . . a relative of his?"

"I'm his daughter."

"Oi," she said, and massaged her forehead with the back of her wrist. "This is heavy. I mean like you live with your dad, right? And . . . ah . . . he didn't tell you he's out on his . . . like he's no longer employed?"

She was getting through to me. It was mutually painful.

"I thought—" And then I remembered seeing Dad at the Sunoco station the week before, when he should have been on the train. It began to make sense, the only thing that did.

"—of tea or something?"

"Excuse me? I wasn't listening," I said.

"Would you like a cup of tea or something? The water's like still hot." Since I was at the end of the line, I sat down and took the cup of tea. Until then I hadn't thought about the return trip. Somehow I expected to dump my problem on Dad and let him take it from there. Infantile.

She fussed around a lot, getting the tea and then some cookies. Finally we were both just sitting there staring at each other across her desk. A sign on it said, "Today is the first day of the rest of your life." "Well, you know, business has really been off. Like *way* off. I mean, how many building starts are there these days, or even renovations, right? I mean where are people supposed to come up with mortgage money? Right? Look at the interest rates. So, you know, your dad, he's—was like a junior partner, and there just aren't enough commissions coming in for three architects. You know where I'm coming from? Like it's a dollars-and-cents-type thing. He's a good architect, really talented, but that's the way it goes. Some firms have gone completely under just here lately."

She finally wound down. I could almost see myself through her square lenses: a sheltered, pampered little suburban type who didn't even know where the food on her table came from, with a father so protective he didn't dare tell her the facts of his life.

"You live some place up in Connecticut, right? I was out in the suburbs once. I forget which one—in Jersey I think it was. It's like . . . a whole different scene. You still in school? What is this, some kind of a holiday?" She checked her calendar, expecting a clue.

"No. I cut school to see my dad."

"Oh wow! You mean he's not home?"

"He always leaves the house at the regular time."

"Then like your mother doesn't know either?" And then I remembered that Mother was taking that real-estate salesmanship course—hoping she could bring in some money. We were a great little family for secrets.

"I suppose she knows, now that I come to think of it," I said. "I better go. I don't want to keep you from your work."

"What work?" she said. "If there was work, your dad would still be here."

"I just wonder where he is. Maybe he's out going to interviews. Maybe he's already got another job . . ."

She was shaking her head and looking at me over the rim of the mug. "Don't get your hopes up. I mean like if he had another job, we'd have heard. He'd have taken his drafting board and like that, but everything's still here. There just aren't any jobs going now."

"But then why does he get dressed up every morning and—"

"They all do it. Even if they don't have interviews to go to. They like kind of try to keep in the rhythm. At first they have résumés printed up. Then they start going to flicks during the day. Some of them drink. They usually end up sitting in the park, if it's a nice day. It's really rough, you know? Like men can't afford to fail. It's like bred into them."

"I wish I knew where he was. I don't even want to say anything to him about . . . what I came to say. I just wish I knew where he was."

"There's a little vest-pocket park down at the end of this block and to the left, uptown. He might be there. A lot of times they go to the nearest place to where they worked. Habit, I guess."

I started to go then, not remembering to say good-bye. But she called out after me, "Say, listen! I don't even know your name."

"Gail."

"Well, listen, Gail, when you see your dad, tell him hi from Connie. I mean if you want him to know you were here. Tell him to hang in there and like that, you know where I'm coming from?"

I found the vest-pocket park. Only a space where they'd torn down a building and tried to get a little grove of trees started. It was mostly pavement and pigeons and people. But only the pigeons were moving. The people were lined up along the park benches, subway-train close. I nearly missed seeing my dad.

He was halfway along a bench, wedged in between two other strangers. If he'd looked up, he'd have seen me only a few yards away beside a clump of gray marigolds. But he was looking at the ground where the pigeons were bobbing around. There was a newspaper folded on his knee, but he wasn't reading it. He wasn't doing anything. I recognized the tie with the small gold stripe in it I'd given him for his birthday. It was like identifying a dead body in a way. This was the man who was going to make all my problems evaporate. I walked on then, hoping he wouldn't look up. To keep his secret from me, he'd need my cooperation. Like Connie said, men can't afford to fail.

I knew if I kept walking uptown and stayed on the same street, I'd get back to Grand Central Station. There didn't seem to be any great rush about it. On one corner there was a bunch of guys standing around the door of an Off-Track Betting place. Why weren't they in school? Why wasn't I?

They were a blur of crushed-velvet wrap-around coats, shades, and platform shoes. One of the guys, no bigger than I was, stepped out in front of me, cupped his hand, wiggling a finger. "Hey, momma, whatcher hurry? Want a little action? Wanna get it on? Wanna—"

I walked around him in the flow of pedestrians. He should have scared me out of my wits. But I nearly went blind with hatred instead. If he had something to prove about himself, what made him think he could use me? Did I owe him something because I was female and he was male?

It was the first time I'd thought anything like that. I wished I'd had something very sharp and very lethal in my hand. I was ready to use it, on anybody. Then suddenly I was starved. I stopped at a Chock full o'Nuts and had two cream cheese sandwiches and an orange drink.

I don't know why I half expected my mother to be meeting all the trains, but I did. She wasn't the first person I saw when I got off at the station though. The first familiar face was Valerie Cathcart's. She was heading home down Meeting Street with an armload of books. School was just out.

Valerie's father's a doctor. That should put her in the middle of the best group in school, but it didn't work that way for her. She was only half in a gang whose every other phrase was "How gross!" and even they could take her or leave her. So she worked in the school office during her free period and built a small empire as the school busybody.

When she spotted me, she broke into a gallop. It was too late to cross the street to avoid a head-on with her. "Jeez,"

Valerie said, puffing up to me, "where you been all day, Gail? Miss Roseberry in the office called your mom third period and I listened on the extension. Your mom was really grossed out. When she found out you weren't in school, she didn't know what to say. Then she called back in about five minutes and asked if Steve Pastorini was in school. But he was. Jeez, where've you been?"

I opened my mouth to tell her. But something else came blurting out. "What business is it of yours? Do I owe you an explanation for everything I do? I'm sick of living in this fishbowl, and I'm sick of rejects like you who get their kicks from listening in on extensions because you don't have a life of your own." We were both breathless when I could stop talking. I seemed to have a lot to say all of a sudden to pathetic Valerie, for all the good it would do.

"How gross," she said, staring at me with her little pig eyes. "How rank. Excuse me for being alive." Her big soft face began to crumple up, and I felt disgusted with myself only because I'd have to apologize to her. But later, not now.

For nearly a half hour after I got home, I thought I wasn't going to get into it with my mother. I'd never skipped school in my life, and I thought the first time ought to be the occasion for some fireworks. But when I came in, only her gaze followed me up the stairs.

It was nearly time for Dad to come home before she cracked my door and actually asked if she could come in. "Want to talk about it?" she said in a neutral voice.

"I went in to New York to see Dad."

"Oh." She hesitated in the doorway for a moment, digesting that. "I suppose we should have told you before. But your dad didn't want you to worry. You know how he always thinks you're still a little girl."

"And you don't?"

"No. I just wish you were, sometimes."

"So do I, sometimes. Maybe that's why I went."

She came all the way into the room then, walking carefully to show we were going to have a conversation, not a confrontation. "It's very hard for him—your dad."

"Yes, I know. I understand."

"And that's why I'm taking this awful real-estate sales course, though I don't suppose it'll do much—"

"Yes, I understand that too. I wish I could say something to Dad. I don't know what, but—"

"Oh no, honey. I wouldn't if I were you. It would just be another burden to him if he thought you knew."

"That's the way we are, isn't it? All three of us. We keep everything locked up tight inside us because . . . because one little leak might cause an explosion, and we'd all go flying apart."

"That's melodramatic," Mother said, "and I don't know what good talking would do. It wouldn't get Neal—your dad—a job, would it? I, for one, would probably get hysterical. I'm near enough that point anyway."

So am I, I thought, trying to reject the idea that I was so much like my mother. "It'll just help your dad if he thinks you're not worrying," she was saying. "You shouldn't be having problems at your age."

"Didn't you have problems at my age?"

It was nearly dark, and she looked young, sitting on my bed with her knees pulled up under her and the crow's feet around her eyes invisible. Usually I hated it when she came in and flopped down on my bed. But this time we were both making allowances. "Oh, I don't know what I was like then. It seems so long ago. It *was* so long ago."

"Mother, I'm going to go out with Steve tomorrow night,

if he's free. You'll be at your class, and Dad will be at his board meeting. I don't feel like staying home alone. I don't want to."

She didn't hear those last words. "Oh, Gail, not on a school night. You know how your dad feels about—"

"You're the one who doesn't want me going out with Steve, Mother. Let's not kid ourselves."

She'd wrinkled my bedspread up into a little fan of pleats, running the edge of her thumbnail down the folds. "All right, we won't kid ourselves about that. I almost wish— I do wish we'd never moved up here. I thought it would be—an ideal environment for you. That we wouldn't have the worry people do, raising a daughter in the city, facing all those problems."

"Why does Steve seem like such a problem to you, Mother? He's not a poor boy from a slum. If anybody's poor, it's us."

"I hope you know how that sounded. Now maybe you can understand why I don't want you telling your dad you know he's out of work."

"Is it because Steve's from an Italian family?"

"I'm not a bigot. And I'm not—Lydia Lawver."

"Then what is it?"

"You take the pill, don't you, Gail." It wasn't a question.

"Yes."

"How long?"

"Since last spring. Right after my birthday. I wasn't sure I could get a prescription if I was under sixteen."

"And you got them from Dr. Cathcart! And he didn't inform me! I think that's . . . unethical."

"No, I didn't get them from him. But I got them in a perfectly safe, legal way."

Mother tried to smooth out the mess she'd made of the

bedspread. "I wish you wouldn't take those pills. You know about the side effects. They're really not sure if there aren't links with blood clots and strokes and heart attacks and—"

"But you take them, Mother. The only difference is yours are in the medicine cabinet in the bathroom, and I keep mine under my scrapbook in that drawer over there where you must have found them."

She looked away then but went on talking as if I hadn't said anything. "Well, then if you really didn't get them from Dr. Cathcart, who on earth did you go to?"

"The Planned Parenthood Organization. Down on Meeting Street."

"Where? You didn't."

"I did."

"But that place is for—for *married* people."

"Not entirely. They have a youth counseling division. Mrs. Raymond who works there says it's the biggest part of the program."

"Now don't start telling me *all* the girls at school are on the pill," she snapped. "Don't tell me since *everybody's* on the pill, *you* have to be too. It's not a *driver's license* or—or—"

"I'm not saying that, Mother. It's just that I'm not the only one."

"Well, is Alison Bremer on them too?"

"I don't know, Mother. But no, I don't suppose she is."

"Did Steve Pastorini—"

"It was my decision. Entirely mine. But I did it because of Steve. That's better than if I'd done it because of . . . a lot of boys, isn't it?" I waited a long time for an answer to that, but I didn't get it.

Instead, Mother said, "Well, tell me how you got them

—the pills. You can't just march in that place and demand a prescription, can you?"

"No. There's a whole procedure. Nobody told me about it, and I was scared when I went in the first night. But the volunteer there, they call them support workers—it was Mrs. Raymond, and she—"

"What Mrs. Raymond?"

"I don't know her first name. She volunteers there in the evening."

"You don't mean Eleanor Raymond in my garden club!"

"Yes, she's the one."

"Why I see Eleanor Raymond every week. She—well, go on."

"She was very helpful. She knew who I was, but she didn't make a big thing about it. We went over the various birth control devices. She had a sort of set patter for it, but left time for me to ask questions. She volunteers there because she wants to help people, Mother."

"Yes . . . I suppose so."

"And then she told me to come back in a week after I'd thought things over. Decided which method I wanted, if any."

"And then you went back there. How did you have the nerve?"

"I just did. And I said I wanted the pill. I had to see a doctor that time. He was volunteering there too. A gynecologist. I don't know where his regular practice is. And after an examination, he gave me a prescription."

"A thorough examination?"

"A pelvic examination. I have the prescription filled at Walton's Drugstore, and I pay for it out of my sitting money."

"So it was as easy as that."

"It wasn't that easy, Mother. It wasn't an easy decision."

"I just don't want you to get hurt," she said. "If you have to . . . experience everything now, what do you have to look forward to?"

The question hung in the air until the phone began to ring. The sound made the glass things on my dressing table vibrate. Three rings, then four before Mother slipped off the bed and went into her room. I heard her pick up the extension and say, "Hello?" in her usual, somewhat brittle voice. "Hello?" she said louder. "Hello? Hello?"

CHAPTER

Seven

Steve had a paper due on Roosevelt and the New Deal, so it was an effort to convince him that we were going out at night in the middle of the week. But I didn't care where. The library would have been as good as anyplace else. Anywhere away from phones. And he was ready to grill me about my unexplained absence on Tuesday. I got off with a half truth, telling him about Dad being out of work. "I was worried about him," I said.

"Is that what's been bothering you lately?"

"Isn't that enough?" I darted off to Gernreich's geometry.

I had it all timed so that he'd pick me up a few minutes after Dad and Mother left. A few minutes, no more. Dad left on schedule, walking down to the Village Hall for his board meeting. But Mother dawdled, changed her clothes twice.

"Come in, Stephen," I heard her say. She must have

seen him coming up the walk and made it to the door before he rang. I was just starting down the stairs. *This is all I need. If she attacks him for being her daughter's seducer.*

But she was on her dignity, with a little added open-mindedness. "We never get to see enough of you, Stephen," she accused kindly. I stopped on the stairs, trying to see Steve through her eyes. How does a plumber's son look to the wife of an unemployed professional man? The class system seemed to be lying in a heap of rubble on the hall rug. I wondered if Mother knew that the Pastorinis were more secure in their world than we were in ours. I wondered if that was a taunt to her. It would have been so much easier for her if Steve had been a sweathog: cigarette dangling from bad teeth, shifty eyes, black leather over bad posture.

But he wasn't that. He was next year's valedictorian who happened to be having a Relationship with her daughter. Puppy love and The Pill. She may have taken it all more seriously that it was. I could see why she was off balance. But I couldn't see Steve through her eyes. I could barely see him through mine. I was beginning to feel pretty cut off from everybody.

The library was closed. A sign on the door said: "Due to continuing budget cuts and increased operating expenses, this library will no longer observe evening hours until further notice."

"The lake?" Steve said. "We'll build a fire in the cabin stove. There's kindling."

"No, I don't think so."

"No, I guess not," he said. "You're someplace where I can't find you." So we drove around, up and down Meeting Street, out along the Woodbury Road and into the country. Past the barn where the Slaneks lived, with trapezoid-shaped windows throwing light across a weedy yard where

Mr. Slanek's welded I-beam sculpture stood around, casting angular shadows.

It was pouring rain, and I was steaming inside my slicker. Once, on a straight stretch of road, Steve reached over and took my hand. I jumped and pulled away without thinking. "It's not you," I tried to explain. "It's me."

We stopped at Friendly's, which was midweek empty. A couple of malteds didn't loosen our tongues. Steve wasn't the type to fill in with easy conversation. I had the feeling he was brooding about his unwritten Roosevelt paper.

It was almost a relief when the door burst open, and a gang of sweathogs, mostly male in black leather, flocked in, streaming rain water and glittering with chrome studs. They staked out three or four booths. Blue air and that eye-cutting sweet pot smell hung over them. They were all heads, of course.

"Okay," the waitress bawled from the safe distance of the soda fountain. "Don't smoke that junk in here. Cigarettes yes. Joints no."

The sweathogs greeted this interruption with a barrage of catcalls, mostly beginning with the word *mother*. There were a couple of girls with them. Girls you sometimes saw at school, but not usually. The loud one was LaVerne Shull who always wore three-quarter-length boots, wide at the tops like a drum majorette's. She withdrew a pack of Kents from her boot top and offered them around to the guys who were smoking their roaches down to hot husks of brown paper.

"Hey? They close school?" LaVerne yelled over the din of the others. "I mean, they close school or sumpin?" She struggled to get the attention of the others who were trying to spell out words on the table with a squeeze bottle of ketchup. "I mean, look there's Steve Pastorini and Little

Miss What's-Her-Name over there. What are *they* doing out on a school night?"

A couple of the guys muttered what we might be doing out on a school night. LaVerne shrieked. She went on and on, trying to draw the gang that was already all over her closer and closer.

"Let's go," I said to Steve.

"That way LaVerne wins," Steve said. "Besides, I grew up with them, every one of them. My people. LaVerne's dad is probably playing pinochle with my dad right now down at the VFW."

I wanted to tell him that he wasn't one of them any more. But I guessed he knew that. The decibel level of LaVerne's shrieks had lowered considerably. Out of the corner of my eye I could see a hand that wasn't hers trailing like a vine in under her blouse.

We left, after a decent interval, if that's the way to put it. But there wasn't anywhere to go, and I was in no hurry to get home. We drove up and down country roads, listening to the windshield wipers. I reached over and took Steve's hand and he held it, loosely.

"Did you know," I said, "we're being followed?"

"What?"

"There's a car way behind us. It's made the last four or five turns we have, and we're not really going in any particular direction."

He glanced in the rear-view mirror. "There's a car back there, but way back. Could have been different cars on different roads."

"No. It's the same one."

"You can't be sure about that, Gail. What's the matter with you?"

"Nothing at all. I'm just telling you somebody's following us, and I thought you'd like to know. Point of interest."

He either didn't believe me or didn't want to, for a mile or so. But then he swung the car suddenly into a side road, so fast we nearly grazed a stone wall. It was a farmer's lane, with a darkened house at the end and a barnlot turn-around. We circled in it, throwing up a wave of mud. He killed the lights, and we sat there in the dark with the rain pounding the hood. There was a car way off on the main road, with headlights low to the ground, fanning out. But it wasn't moving.

We were there a long time, sitting apart, until Steve was as nervous as I was. He flicked on the lights and gunned off down the lane. The other car in the distance leaped forward a second later. By the time we got down to the end of the lane it had roared by on the road. Its tail lights were only red pinpoints ahead of us when we turned out of the lane. Then it was gone.

"It was really traveling," Steve muttered. "I didn't think any of LaVerne's mob had a car that fast."

"Maybe they don't," I said.

"Hand it over to me right now!" I snapped my fingers right under Alison's nose. "Don't even unfold it." I'd come down the hall Thursday morning just in time to see her pull a note out of my locker vent.

"Oh, Gail," she said, trying to look superior and concerned all at once, "why don't you just throw it away? Why give anybody the satisfaction of reading it and getting all upset? It's probably some, oh, I don't know, some scramble-brained girl who's jealous and trying to do a number on your head. Not worth fussing about."

"How would you feel if somebody was doing this particular number on *your* head, Alison? Or couldn't anything like that ever possibly happen to *you*? Just give it to me." I had to take it out of her hand. I'd have fought her for it, torn her hair out, like LaVerne Shull would. When I unfolded it, Alison turned away.

I'M STILL WATCHING YOU. AND I'M GETTING CLOSER, YOU LITTLE...

It was almost the same as the first note. He'd said it all before. He'd been living with his same psycho plans ever since. And so had I.

I fumbled it into my book bag, wedged it between Wood's *Masters of English Literature* and Waddell's *Basic Principles of Plane Geometry*. I turned around with a mask of calm on my face. "Look how cool I am, Alison. Like you said before, it never happened." My head throbbed, and I felt a flash of hate for her. Because it wasn't happening to her. Because she knew. Because she was saying all the wrong things—inadequate words like *fuss*. What did I want her to say? That twisted letter writers like this one are all talk, that they only harm themselves? I wouldn't have believed her.

I gagged then and thought I was going to lose my breakfast. But I kept swallowing and swallowing until my eyes burned and my face felt like paper.

Sonia outdid herself that morning. She was wearing a Spanish shawl that looked like it had come off the top of a piano. It was embroidered in limes and pineapples in living color, with a fringe. She'd circled it around her smooth hair and draped it over one shoulder, pinned with a velvet rose. And under it she wore basic black, something like an evening gown, with beads following the seams on the skirt down to high-heeled suede boots. "She's really going too far," Alison said, though she only glanced at Sonia and kept a worried eye on me. Sonia swept past us on a cloud of Evening in Paris cologne.

It was the monthly Arts Assembly day. I marched through it like a sleepwalker and right into the auditorium for the double period after lunch. We were supposed to sit according to home rooms, but everybody juggled around to be with friends. Steve had staked out a couple of seats for us over on one side in case the performance of the day was the Oldfield String Quartet or Girls' Junior Glee or something like that. Steve generally liked to sit by a window where he could see to read in case the culture was too home-grown. "Wake me up if it turns out to be Beverly Sills or the Vienna Philharmonic. Otherwise, don't." I could think of a way of waking him up. I could reach down in my book bag and hand him the latest note. But I didn't.

The teachers started up the side aisles with poles to pull the black-out shades down. "A flick," Steve muttered out of the side of his mouth. "Hope it's not the product of a hand-held camera."

In the gloom, somebody scurried in and flopped down in the empty seat beside me. Anything like that made me jump out of my skin. But when I turned to see who it was, Valerie Cathcart's moonface was staring inches from me. She flinched when she recognized me, and even started out of her seat. "No, wait, Val. Listen, I'm sorry I bit your head off the other day down by the station. I was in a funky mood."

"Oh, it's all right," Valerie said in the tone of one who's had a lot of forgiving to do in her time. "What's the movie, do you know? They don't even know in the office, either that or they're not telling. If it was about, you know, personal hygiene or something in that area, they wouldn't be showing it to the guys and *us*, at the same time, would they?"

"I doubt it, Val. So don't get your hopes up."

"Oh, but I didn't mean— Oh, it's starting now. Look that's Miss Venable on the stage." It took Valerie to tell me who Miss Venable was. She'd just come that fall to be a guidance counselor. And unless you were Valerie Cathcart or a juvenile offender, you wouldn't have run into her. Miss Venable had that I'm-fighting-for-control look that new faculty members have until they're broken in.

"All right now," she shouted. "Let's settle down and have some order here!" The spotlight scanned the stage in front of the screen, trying to find her. She was sidestepping herself, trying to get into the light. "Let's have less unnecessary conversation, and I mean it!" A lot of the conversation came from people wondering who she was.

She was definitely fresh out of graduate school—somewhere in inner-city New York probably. No makeup, lank hair, yesterday's blouse working up out of her belt. She kept running the side of her thumb down her cheek to get the hair out of her face. Unfolding a page, she began to read her prepared speech.

"Boys and girls, the principal has asked me to introduce this monthly Arts Assembly which I understand is one of Oldfield High's most time-honored traditions. Today, in place of a live performance"—there came a series of sharp high shrieks from the back of the auditorium along sweat-hogs' row; they were clearly LaVerne Shull's, who must have been giving a live performance of her own—"we have a special treat of particular significance to our school.

"The film we are all about to enjoy, which has been obtained through the good offices of the Museum of Modern Art archives in New York, reaches well back into the annals of cinematographic history. It is the art form of an earlier era almost miraculously preserved. And so I invite you all to sit back—quietly—and enjoy a movie, filmed in 1926, which I feel sure needs no further introduction."

Miss Venable tried for a quick but controlled exit off the stage. There was a tremendous burst of applause, but she missed the irony of it. A few penetrating whistles and a voice yelling, "Give the little lady a big hand," sent her in full flight.

"Who is that woman and what is she talking about?" Steve said, making a steeple of his fingers in front of his nose and settling down in the seat.

The film broke a couple of times during the credits and seemed to catch fire once. The color went from grainy gray to muddy yellow bubbles. I think the title was *Roses in Ruin*, but I can't be sure. The only sound was the whir of the projector, since it was obviously from the age of silent movies. Still, there were a few loud demands to turn up the volume, and Val said, "Oh dear, I guess it's going to be historical."

It was, in its way. The lighting was so bad that it took a while to see that this was a fancy-dress party scene with people moving like painted dolls all over a ballroom in a cheek-to-cheek dance. I suppose originally there was live musical accompaniment to add realism. An organ or something. But now they danced in silence and the whites of their eyes and their hands were deathly pale. The chandeliers tinkled without any noise over their heads, and a breeze blew the long lace curtains on French doors.

"I'm not getting the deeper meaning of this," Steve muttered.

The party scene was interrupted by a printed card that read,

A BAL MASQUE AT THE CHATEAU OF
PRINCE TALLEYRAND-PERIGORD ON A BALMY SPRING
EVENING FIFTY THOUSAND NIGHTS AGO

The natives in the auditorium were getting restless. But the ballroom scene returned, and the dancers separated. A young girl was discovered standing under the chandelier, holding her mask well away from her face so the camera could zoom in on her.

In a way she was ridiculous. A flat-chested 1920s flapper dressed up in an eighteenth-century gown with a low neckline. She was the only one without a powdered wig, and her hair was lacquered glossy black and looped with pearls. And she was sensationally beautiful. Black lips and hair and a black beauty mark at her temple for the right period touch. She gazed around the crowded ballroom with her hand at her neck in a wonderfully graceful gesture. I realized I was trying to copy her, reaching up to the green heart I wore on the chain.

The film jumped off its sprockets or something and started fluttering. But the audience was half grabbed by then and started a clapping rhythm. When the picture came back, the girl was whirling around the room, first with one partner and then another. Fat ones, thin ones, one who must have been the king of France.

"I'm not sure," Steve mumbled again, "but I don't think they did the tango at the court of Louis the Sixteenth."

But he was watching the girl too. The way her silver skirts swept over the floor. The tiny curved heels of her dancing slippers. The line of her neck as her head drew back to hear the compliments whispered into her ear. Her presence seemed to leap off the cracked old film and crackle with life.

There was a lot of nonsense acted out in mime. Something about a diamond bracelet lost and old ladies in stiff brocaded skirts screaming soundlessly and clutching at their dangling ear rings. And servants being accused.

Naturally there was a thief outside the palace, masked too, but for a different reason. He was climbing around on the rose trellis and swinging from grapevines—with a diamond bracelet dangling out of his pocket. I think the reels got reversed because suddenly the beautiful girl was standing alone on the terrace with her back to the room full of dancers. She was gazing up at the moon, turning her almond-shaped face up to show that long white swan neck again. Instead of a mask, she was holding a fan. She worked it in an underwater motion, touching the hollow of her neck with it, closing it and running it down the white curve of her arm. She seemed to know all about charisma before there was a word for it.

Then the masked thief swung onto the terrace, and his very white teeth gleamed as he stood there, boots wide apart and hands on hips, devouring her with his masked eyes. When she saw him, she tried to hide behind her fan—another ridiculous, beautiful gesture. Her eyes got enormous as she looked into the camera, begging us to save her.

But there wasn't anything we could do, though even Steve was almost up on the edge of his seat by then. There was a lot more business between the thief and the maiden, including her ripping off his mask which was supposed to reveal him as the illegitimate brother of some duke. Then he swept her up in his arms, and they flew away from the terrace on another convenient vine.

The scene jerked to a rose garden with the moonlight wet as water all around, and the camera concentrating on a statue of Cupid in the middle of a fountain. The girl resisted the thief, broke away from him, and began to run up and down the avenues of rose bushes. The camera cut from her running, stumbling, running again, to the thief standing perfectly still, laughing silently. Only then did I stop enjoying it. She could run and run, but she couldn't escape.

The film blurred again, and she was in his arms, thrashing away at him with her fan until it shattered in a shower of sticks. The two of them fell in slow motion to the ground, and the rose bushes seemed to grow up around them.

This must have been before the days of censorship. The girl tore the thief's white shirt off his shoulders and clawed long black gashes in his back. His head was buried in her breast, his hands wrenching away the ballooning sleeves from her arms.

The camera only caught the top of his curly head to reveal her face above it. The maiden being ravished. Terror gradually replaced by passion. Her eyes slowly closed, and her lashes lay fringed on her cheeks. A small secret smile played across her lips. The stone Cupid on the fountain above them came miraculously alive then and shot an arrow in the direction of the moon.

The auditorium lights went up, and the crowd went fairly wild. It wasn't your usual Arts Assembly, and the seduction scene had overstimulated several people. We were all mystified about why they'd shown it. Thinking it was over, I reached down for my book bag, and reality rushed back when I remembered the note. Something clicked in my mind then, very gently. Some connection between the fantasy trip of the movie and the trapped feeling when it was over.

But it wasn't over. Miss Venable jumped up and yelled for us to sit down and be quiet. A total hush fell over the crowd anyway, because Sonia Slanek walked out of the wings and across to center stage.

In some quarters, Sonia's eternal camp was always good for a laugh. But this time she was having her moment of glory. Her clinging black gown and gaudy shawl carried out the theme of the film perfectly. She must have planned it that way. And when she got up to the microphone, she turned big, over-made-up eyes on us, using them just like a silent movie star would. You could have heard a pin drop. Watching her was a major school pastime. But we were about to hear her too.

She tossed the fringes of her shawl over one shoulder and opened her Cupid's-bow lips. "The film you've just seen," she said in a perfectly ordinary voice, "broke all attendance records when it was premiered at the Roxy Theater in New York. My father was instrumental in discovering this print of it which has lain, mislabeled for a half century, in the museum archives. It's characteristic of the films of that time, when the fashion for screen heroes was set by Douglas Fairbanks and Rudolph Valentino and then endlessly copied by other actors.

"In a way it describes an art lost when sound began to be added to movies in the following year. The performers of the silent era were called upon to devise an entire system of body language to express their emotions and to advance the fairly simple plots of the totally visual stories."

"She's good," Steve said, on one side of me.

From the other Valerie whispered, "She sounds real normal, kind of like a teacher."

"The female stars of the 1920s," Sonia continued, "are often remembered as awkward flappers, doing the Charleston, with their stockings rolled below the knees and their hair chopped off and shingled up the back.

"A closer look at an original source reveals a very different kind of female ideal. And it suggests the considerable artistry required of the performer working in a silent medium."

Then Sonia dropped her bombshell. "A distinction of

this school is that one of our teachers was the beautiful and talented actress of the movie we've just seen. Our drama teacher, Dovima Malevich."

There was a weird rushing sound as a general gasp swept through the auditorium. The spotlight hit the front row where Madam Malevich was sitting. She was humped over in her seat, wedged in between two other teachers who didn't have homerooms.

The teachers on either side of her stood then and began to applaud, looking down at the wide white part in her black hair and smiling kindly. Then we were all applauding and starting to stand up. Sweathogs and high-level heads. And bustasses and ninth-graders who hadn't even discovered her yet. The cheer leaders cheered. And people who'd snickered at her were clapping instead. A star was born in our midst, never mind that it was a half century late. It was almost like discovering that the little old man who'd been teaching history was Woodrow Wilson in disguise.

The music teacher, Mr. Bryant, shouted "Brava!" and then everyone did. And somebody called for a speech. But Madam Malevich didn't rise for a long time. She only sat there, looking very small and farther away than she had on the screen. And we all stared at the knot of black hair that rested on her rounded back.

But finally one of the teachers bent down, whispered something, and offered her an arm. She stood up, and the applause whipped into a frenzy. It seemed to charge through her. She stood taller and walked around the orchestra pit toward the stage, shrugging off all help on the steps.

As she walked across to the mike, she was her usual, beaky-nosed, pigeon-shaped self. She shuffled in her space shoes. But we were all seeing her with different eyes now.

She stood in front of the mike until we were all as silent as her film. Her eyes were the eyes of the girl we'd just seen on the screen. "I vas silent screen actress," she began, "so I better be silent now so as not to destroy the mood. Yes, I vas young once, as you see. I lived out my dreams and then I outlived them. It is what happens to everybody.

"But a moment like today? No. That don't happen to everybody. I am grateful from my heart to Sonia Slanek and her father and to all those who bring back a moment or two from my youth to share wiz you who are young now. And so Dovima says no more, for she weeps."

And she did. Dark stains formed in the pockets under her eyes as her mascara flowed down her face. She walked blinking across the stage and into the darkness of the wings. Her timing was right on as usual, but this time it wasn't a performance.

Valerie strangled over a dry sob. I was trying to keep the tears back. And Steve took off his glasses and began giving them a vigorous polish.

CHAPTER

Eight

The school buzzed all Thursday about Madam Malevich. Since it was Sonia Slanek who'd discovered her, people were buzzing about her too. When Sonia came to school, instead of watching her walk past them, people stopped her in the hall, congratulating her. But Sonia had retreated into her shell again, looking impatient at the attention. It was her moment to belong, but her brown lips just smiled, and her butterfly eyes fluttered away.

"Wouldn't you think she'd want a little credit?" Alison was saying. "I mean who else would bother to dig around and find out who Malevich really is, or was? And then have the contacts to turn up that old film and all."

"I doubt if she was doing it for our benefit. I expect she did it for Madam Malevich. Somehow I don't think Sonia needs us."

"Everybody needs somebody," Alison said, very definite. "I mean, you never know when you'll need a friend."

That must have stuck in my mind. That business about friendship. I usually met up with Alison before third period study hall. Our paths crossed outside the counseling wing door. It was propped open, and I looked inside. I'd never been in there. In a cubicle across the outer office, Miss Venable, the new guidance counselor, was at her desk.

And then Alison came bustling along. "Is there time to go to the john before the bell? My hair's a—"

"Alison, I ought to talk to a counselor."

"What about?" She kept looking over my head, searching for the hall clock.

"You know what about. The latest note."

"You don't still have it, do you?" she said, finally looking at me. "You're not carrying it around, are you?"

"Yes. Come in with me." She took a step back.

"What about study hall?" she said.

"What about it? I need to have somebody with me." I knew the excuses were bubbling up in her brain, so I said, "You never know when you'll need a friend."

She walked just behind me into the counseling wing, muttering "This is pointless." I stepped right up to Miss Venable's desk, willing Alison to stay with me.

"Do you two have appointments?"

"Are you a doctor?" I asked. Alison moaned. I was getting a fresh mouth for the first time in my life.

Miss Venable had very straight hair, 1960s-long. It tangled with her glasses frames where it was tucked behind her ears. She had the clinical, cosmetic-free face of a guidance counselor, but she looked very young. I wondered if that was good or bad. "I beg your pardon?" she said.

"Do you have to have an appointment to see a counselor? I have a problem."

"Oh." She moved a paperweight from one side of her blank blotter to another. "Getting a referral from a teacher is the standard procedure."

"This isn't a standard problem." Her gaze shifted back

and forth between Alison and me. "It's my problem. This is a friend of mine."

"Oh." She inspected me then. I could hear her mind ticking over. Combed hair, clean, natural color. Fresh blouse. Small green heart on thin gold chain, nothing clanky. All-wool skirt, not cheap. "Sit down," she said, revolving in her chair. "I'll pull your file. Name?" There was only one chair, and I sat down in it. Alison seemed to hang suspended in the doorway of the cubicle, ready to bolt. *If she goes, she goes,* I thought.

"Osburne, Gail. Eleventh grade." Miss Venable leafed through my file twice, looking for a history of maladjustment. "Let's see," she said, tapping a pencil against her teeth. "You've had your Kuder Preference, of course, and your PSAT last year. Right up at the top in verbal and reading comprehension. Slightly better than so-so in math skills. You'll be taking SAT's this winter, but no problem there. You test well. Straight college prep program. Were you thinking about Boards or an early admissions program? Because if you are, there's a college counselor for that and you ought to see—"

"No, I wasn't thinking about that."

"Well, then, what is it?" She pushed her chair back from her desk a few inches. *Don't you retreat from me too,* I thought.

"I'm being bothered by somebody."

"How do you mean?"

"Notes, phone calls."

"I don't know anything about any phone calls," Alison said suddenly.

"Phone calls," I said. "He seems to know where I am all the time, especially when I'm by myself."

"What's his name?"

"I don't know."

"But you said *he*. Are you sure it's a boy?"

"No," Alison said.

"I'm pretty sure it's a boy," I said, looking up at Alison. She was fidgeting, shifting her books from arm to arm.

"Well, you're a very attractive girl—both of you are," Miss Venable said. "You have to expect some . . . attention that isn't always too welcome . . ."

How would you know? I wondered. My hands were getting damp. "It's more serious than that."

"We all fantasize a little. It's nothing to be ashamed of. We all daydream, don't we?"

"I wouldn't bring my daydreams to a counselor," I said. "I'd be pretty careful to keep them to myself."

"Well, then, surely you have some idea who he might be. Do you have a boy friend?"

"Yes," I said, "but he's not a sex maniac." Alison moaned again.

"There's no need to go overboard," Miss Venable said. I hadn't meant to show that last note to anybody. But I was still carrying it around, shifting it from book bag to purse. At that point it was pressed in the pages of *Fifty Great Scenes for Student Actors*.

"Maybe you better take a look at this evidence," I said, handing the note to her. She took it out of my hand and unfolded it.

Alison swooped down on me and began to whisper urgently into my ear, "Listen, Gail, I really, I mean *really* don't want to be here. This is *embarrassing*. And I ought to get to study hall. I mean I don't have any legitimate reason for cutting."

"Then go," I said out loud, not looking at her. Miss Venable gave her a long look, watching as Alison fled. *Why doesn't she keep reading that note?* I wondered.

"Who was that girl?"

"It doesn't matter," I said. "Somebody who doesn't want to get involved. Did you read the note?"

"I read enough."

"I don't know what to do." My voice cracked, but Miss Venable didn't seem to notice. She had something else on her mind.

"Is this some kind of a put-on?" She was trying to stare me down. "Tell me the truth. Did you and that other girl cook this up between you to spring on me—just because I'm new here?"

My knees were wobbly when I stood up. It was like those dreams when you're running and not getting anywhere and screaming but no one hears. "Give me the note," I said. "I wanted help, not a lie-detector test. I've got enough troubles without you. It's just like I always thought. You people know all about Kuder Preference Tests and the rest of that useless junk, but when it comes to a real problem you can't handle it!"

She must have seen something terrible in my face, looming over her desk. My hand was out for the note, but it was shaking, and I couldn't control it. I seemed to be getting her attention, now that I was acting wild and maladjusted.

"Wait. Sit down." She pressed her fingertips against her forehead. "I'm sorry. I shouldn't have accused you. It's against all my training. It was just . . . that note, it's . . . *psychotic*. It's not just childish nastiness, it's *deeply disturbed*. I realize it's . . . authentic. And we're going to . . . to do something. You wait here. I'll be right back." She was out of the room faster than Alison. I didn't know where she was going.

The clock kept jumping. The period was half over. I thought it'd probably be doing Venable a favor if I just went on to study hall. I'd have bet anything she'd never come near me again. I seemed to be learning a lot about human psychology all at once—abnormal and normal.

It was pointless, as Alison had said. But I decided to wait Miss Venable out. Five minutes. Ten. Then a man stepped into the cubicle. It was Mr. Sampson. He was a counselor too, as well as Dean of Boys. People interested in school politics said he really ran the place on behalf of the invisible principal. And Mr. Sampson had been there since the dark ages, appointed like Madam Malevich by the long dead senior Mrs. Lawver.

He looked enough like a principal to be one, tall and stoop-shouldered. He was the only male I hadn't been worrying about lately, mainly because I hadn't happened to run across him in the hall. He held the note in his hand.

"You're Gail Osburne? I hope you won't mind if I . . . step in on Miss Venable's behalf. This note you showed her . . . well, it's pretty strong stuff. I'm afraid she thinks she bungled her attempt to help you. She's new this year, you know."

There was a long pause then. What was I supposed to say? Was it my fault she couldn't handle her job? "I can understand," he finally went on, "that you would bring this situation to a woman. However, I hope you won't mind if I offer to help. Since the note seems to come from a boy, and I'm Dean of Boys. You understand?"

I nodded.

"You know, boys at your age are mostly all talk."

"Even if they are, why should I have to listen?"

"Well, now . . . Gail, that's a good point. A very good point. And you shouldn't have to. And I can see you're not the kind of girl who . . . well, you're just not that kind of girl. You know what I mean?"

"No."

"Well, let's skip that. Usually in a situation of this type, the girl knows the boy who's ... giving her trouble. I expect if you really give it some thought, you can come up with the name of a boy who's perhaps ... hanging around where you are, making remarks, that kind of thing."

"No, I can't. Besides, if he was saying these things to my face, why would he need the notes and the phone calls?"

Without answering that, Mr. Sampson said, "What are the phone calls like?"

"Usually just silence. Once a filthy word. And usually when I'm someplace alone."

"That doesn't give us much to work on, does it?" The expression on his face brightened when the passing bell rang. "I'll tell you what I'll do. I'll have a word with two or three of our problem boys. They're in and out of my office half the time as it is. And then maybe—"

"Are these guys you're talking about able to write—or even spell a note like that?" I asked him.

He edged off Miss Venable's desk and straightened his tie. "You better skip along to third period now. No sense making me write you out a late pass, is there?"

I was way down the hall before I realized Mr. Sampson had kept the note.

How can I explain where my head was by Saturday night, and I was sitting at Mrs. Montgomery's? It's so easy now to look back and see that every step I took was wrong. Quicksand comes to mind.

I blew an entire day marveling at Miss Venable. This practically adult woman, drawing a salary, who could jump up from her desk and go hide, probably in the faculty women's lounge, while somebody else got rid of me.

But by Friday afternoon I'd psyched myself into a totally unreal world. No phone calls all week. Both notes out of my hands. Alison had said it back at the beginning: *it never happened*. For about five minutes I thought about quitting the baby-sitting job for Mrs. Montgomery. No sense in tempting fate ... or whoever it was. Except he didn't exist any more. Besides, I should be earning more and spending less.

Friday night Steve and I went out and did all the things he hates most, and I had a great time because there were people everywhere we went. Herds of them. Droves of them. We went to the football rally, and it poured rain so hard they couldn't even get the bonfire lit.

Still, the rah-rah girls got up on the wet stage and did their pompom numbers, and the football team did their thing, completely suited up and bursting through big hoops of soggy paper. "Do we let a little rain dampen our spirits?" "NO!" the crowd roared. "Does our team play their best in the mud?" "YES!" the crowd roared. I tried to shelter Steve with half my slicker, but he only stood there, looking red-nosed and rat-drowned.

Then we went to Friendly's, and everybody was there, smoking up a storm, building pyramids of soda spoons, leaving nickel tips in the bottoms of sundae glasses. The jukebox throbbed "Why Can't We Be Friends?" by War.

Alison and Phil were there, in a booth on the other side of the counter, and she and I sent our old upbeat signals back and forth through the smoke from a variety of weeds. I'd already decided not to hold it against her—that running off to leave me in Miss Venable's incompetent hands. When you've got a problem your friends can't face, you become a ... leper. Maybe I'd only dragged Alison in because I was jealous of her too perfect life style. Subconscious motivation. Case closed.

When we got home, Steve kissed me goodnight. A nice, chaste kiss, nearly missing my lips entirely. Or did I turn away at the last second? We seemed to be back at the beginning again, without the thrill of discovery. I hung my wet slicker on a hanger out in the hall where it would drip on the tiles. Then I walked serenely past the phone and up the stairs to bed.

But on Saturday night it all fell apart. Mrs. Montgomery and the coach hadn't been gone fifteen minutes, and the world seemed to be tearing at the seams. The house creaked and moaned on a windless night. The mantel clock throbbed like "The Tell-Tale Heart." Even the fireplace tools seemed to rattle in their brass stand. I stood in the archway looking out to the hall where I could see that yes, yes, yes, I'd put the chain on the door, and no, no, no, the phone wasn't about to ring.

I waited another hour with the two dreaming Montgomery kids fast asleep right above my head, in my care. But something was wrong with the mantel clock. It was ticking its heart out, and yet only ten minutes had passed. Not an hour. Ten minutes.

I flew at the phone. Why hadn't I thought of this before? If I kept talking on the phone, it couldn't ring. You couldn't just leave it off the hook, it squawked. I dialed Steve's number, and Mrs. Pastorini answered. I stuttered, but she seemed willing to wait. Steve was out, gone all the way to Norwalk with his dad to take delivery on a shipment of pipe, probably wouldn't be back before midnight. Did I want him to call me, even that late?

No. Yes. "Yes, Mrs. Pastorini, as soon as he—no, would you ask him to come over to Mrs. Montgomery's as soon as he gets home, no matter when?"

That would have taken courage if I'd been thinking. Asking a boy's mother to tell him to come to the house where you're baby-sitting. But Mrs. Pastorini only said she'd give him the message. And as I hung up, she said, "Bye now, honey," which is probably what she always said at the end of a phone call.

I eased the receiver back on the cradle, and the minute —no, the second I took my hand away, the phone rang. It was almost supernatural. When the receiver was next to my ear again, it was still warm.

And there at the other end was the most terrifying voice I'd ever heard. Sometimes I still hear it, just as I'm going to sleep or in a room that's too quiet. It wasn't quite human. Neither male nor female. A high, hollow voice, someone crying out the words from the inside of a bell. Disguised, falsetto, almost like a child shrieking. But more controlled than that because I understood every word.

"ARE YOU IN THE HOUSE ALONE?"

There was a sobbing, whistling laugh. It was too terrible to be real. And too real to be a horror movie. If there'd been a hundred people in the house with me, all ready to defend the place, I'd still have been paralyzed.

And then that voice again.

"ARE YOU IN THE HOUSE ALONE?"

I remember walking up the stairs next, like an old woman, one step at a time, resting on the landing, bending because my stomach felt cramped. My one thought was to check on the kids, make sure they were all right. They were both asleep. I sat down on the junior bed of the older one and looked down at her. She was sleeping furiously, with her thumb held lightly in her mouth by the edges of her teeth. I concentrated on her name. I hardly knew them. They were always asleep. This was

Angie. The little one in the bed with the sides was Melissa
—Missy.

"Don't you worry, Angie. I'm here to protect you. You
too, Missy." I whispered to keep from waking them. I
don't know how long I sat on Angie's bed, looking back
and forth from her to Missy. And then I knew I wasn't
going to make it through the evening.

I ran out of the room, down the stairs, and began rum-
maging in the drawer of the telephone table. The scrap of
paper with the Previously Marrieds Club number was at
the bottom. I lifted the receiver, and tried to dial, hoping
I could page Mrs. Montgomery. My finger skipped out of
the dial, and I started over. The chimes on the front door
rang then. I heard a scuffling sound outside, someone wip-
ing his feet on the welcome mat.

"*Steve!*" I dropped the phone and ran across to the front
door. The chain lock jammed, then loosened, then jammed
again. Then it fell free, and I threw the door open.

But it wasn't Steve. No, the time was all wrong. It
couldn't have been Steve.

CHAPTER

Nine

I know now how stupid it was to throw that door open. But it already seemed to be past midnight. Steve might have come back from Norwalk. When I saw Phil Lawver instead, I was only a little surprised.

He was standing under the light with the collar of his suede jacket turned up all around. "Oh hi, Gail," he said in his usual drawl. "Listen, is Alison here?"

"No, is she supposed to be?"

"Well, that's just it," he said. "I don't know. I can't figure out where she is, and I don't like her roaming around after dark. Anything could happen. Can I use your phone to call and see if she's home?"

I pointed out the phone to him and walked into the living room, thinking that at least the phone couldn't ring for the next minute or so. I was standing on the hearth rug, checking the time on the mantel clock—it was nearly midnight—when I heard the voice again.

The same shrill sexless voice, ringing like a bell. But it was there in the room with me.

"ARE YOU IN THE HOUSE ALONE?"

It ended in a kind of giggle.

I whirled around, and Phil was standing in the archway. His hands were stuck in the back pockets of his cords, and he'd dropped his jacket on the floor. He was the picture of coolness, and grinning, which was a rare thing for him.

"Had you fooled, didn't I, Gail? The sound was probably even weirder over the phone. Wasn't it weirder?"

"Oh, no, Phil. Has it been you, all along? That's . . . cra—"

"I've been keeping tabs on you. Checking you out pretty close. The phone calls just to keep in touch. And the notes. It was a lot of trouble, actually, for a cheap little— but then I guess you know what I think about you. And the hanky-panky out at the lake with Steve. That was fairly disgusting too. You've taken up a lot of my time, more than you're worth, actually. Something ought to be done about girls like you, Gail. As my mother would say, you tend to lower the tone."

"Phil, look, I think you've got a problem, and—"

"Don't use the psychological approach with me, Gail. You're more the physical type anyway, aren't you?"

Phil Lawver was moving toward me, edging across the room as he talked, gliding around the coffee table. And there wasn't any place for me to go, if I could have moved. I still couldn't quite absorb it. He looked so much the way he always looked. The face crisply chiseled, the panther grace of his movements. I don't think we'd ever really had anything to say to each other, never been in the same room alone. Till now. And he was getting closer. And it didn't matter that I knew who he was.

"Do you?"

"What—what did you say?"

"You're not paying attention, Gail. I said, you don't save it all for Pastorini, do you? Be a shame if you did. He's not worth it. He's nothing. He doesn't exist."

"Phil, listen. Tell me one thing. Have you been drinking?"

"Why, no, Gail. Not a drop. I planned all along to be sober for this evening, and I am. I always knew it would be an evening, a quiet one. I've been very patient in my planning. I've been very patient with you."

He was nearer than I knew when he lunged at me, hooking his ankle around mine. I fell flat on my back in front of the fire screen. Then he dropped down and pinned both my wrists above my head with his hands. "I'm in very good shape, Gail. It comes from clean living, which you wouldn't know anything about. So if you struggle much, you might wish you hadn't. Of course, if struggling turns you on, go right ahead. But I can't be responsible. I can't be responsible for anything."

He pushed his face against the side of my head and whispered into my ear, "And don't worry. I don't want you to do anything you haven't already done. Just look at it this way, Gail. You've had more experience in certain matters than I have. And this is your chance to share it."

A voice from somewhere in my subconscious sounded then, telling me to jam my knee into his groin. I made a feeble attempt, with his full weight tense and flat against me. "Ah, no, Gail, you don't want to try anything like that. Nothing rough. Just think of me as Pastorini. He doesn't go in for the rough stuff, does he? Let's both enjoy this, why not? You've already lost what you've got to lose."

My mind was starting to withdraw from his words just as the tone of them began to get syrupy. I thought of the kids upstairs and how screaming would scare them. I tried to remember what time it was. I thought about dying, but that was just a momentary blackness. "Alison ... so pure ... not like you ... but you ... want me? Don't you? I could have any girl I looked at, but..."

My back arched when he grabbed the front of my shirt and ripped it. The buttons rattled down on the tiles in front of the fire screen. "First of all, let's get rid of this." He grabbed the green heart that was lying against my throat and jerked it off the chain, throwing it over his shoulder.

Both my hands were free in the moment he took to pull his sweater off over his head. But I was afraid to try and dig my nails into his face. *Go for the eyes*, that subconscious voice said again. But he'd have caught my arm before I could raise it. And anyway, I was too terrified. This was the worst, and it was happening. All his promises were coming true, and my silence had been helping him all along.

"I figured you wouldn't have a bra on, Gail. Alison ... Alison ... she always has a bra on, I think. But you're a far cry from Alison, aren't you?"

I guess I should have kept talking, trying to make him hear. But I couldn't think of the right words. And I knew he was long past any reasoning I could think of. He pulled my Levi's down. I felt the floor freezing cold under me. And while he fumbled with his own belt, my hand brushed the base of the stand that held the fireplace tools, the little brass shovel and the broom and the poker.

I made a grab for it, and it fell over, crashing on the tiles. Phil flattened himself on me, and I could feel his body slick with sweat. He slammed his forearm against my throat. But without being able to see anything except for the madness in his eyes, I felt for the handle on the poker, and my hand closed over it. "Lie still, Gail," he said in a soft, dreamy voice, "or I'll have to hurt you more than I'm planning to."

I had one chance to bring the poker up and hit him in the side of the head. *I hope I kill him.* I brought it up, but it only grazed his shoulder. He was up in a sudden crouch, and I remembered the lightning moves he made on the squash court. He twisted the poker out of my hand, looked down at me, surprised, even shocked, and said, "You ... you ... were going to—to try ..." The last thing I remember is the poker in Phil's hand and the way the muscle rippled in his naked shoulder when he brought his arm back in a sportsmanlike backhand just before he swung it down at my temple.

CHAPTER

Ten

I thought I heard a man crying first. It could have been days later. A light glared somewhere overhead, hurting my eyes. There were screens all around, separating me from a lot of rubber-soled footsteps. The place had a hospital smell. A plastic tube was sticking into my hand and snaking off somewhere. It didn't hurt, but it looked like it ought to.

Someone was standing beside the table, holding my other hand. I thought I should say something to him. *"You're* not crying, are you?"

"No, I'm not." He was in a white coat like a doctor and had a rumpled, late-night face.

"What's that tube in my hand for?"

"It's just what we call a 'keep-open' I.V. in case we need to give you fluids—a standard procedure. I expect you have a headache, don't you?"

"How did you know that?"

"Somebody hit you just over your right eyebrow, and

you're getting a nice black eye from it. We've already taken skull X rays and have had to put a few stitches in. Do you feel like talking? If you do, I'll know you're really awake."

Then I knew I was awake, and it wasn't a dream. I even remembered what happened, up to a point. I even knew what I didn't remember. "Am I in Oldfield Hospital?"

"Yes. I'm the emergency room physician. I know Dr. Cathcart takes care of your family, but I'd like to look after you if you don't mind. And I'll be having another doctor see you."

"I guess that's all right. How did I get here?"

"Well, I didn't admit you, but there are several people in the waiting room outside. I expect your parents brought you in."

"Oh no," I said. I tried to shake my head, but there seemed to be a heavy stone lying on my forehead, just above my right eye. "I was at Mrs. Montgomery's, baby-sitting, and I opened the door, and he came in."

There was a space between the tall white screens, and somebody stepped in. It occurred to me then that except for some kind of extra-short hospital gown, I felt naked under the sheet. The emergency room doctor—What was his name? Had we been introduced? Dr. X, I presume— Dr. X laid my hand down gently on the edge of the table and said something quietly to the man who'd come in. Something to do with the fact that I was lucid.

Voices mumbled, and the light over the table was dazzling. I couldn't think about anything but my head, which felt too heavy to lift, and I wondered if this hospital dispensed aspirin.

"Is it still night?" I said, but Dr. X was gone, and the other man was standing there instead.

"Yes," he said, "just after one. Don't you know me, Gail? We've met before." There was an image floating before my good eye. I did know who he was. I just couldn't place him. "Dr. Reynolds. I'm a gynecologist, and I saw you before—at Planned Parenthood."

"Oh. Yes. You're the one with—"

"With what?"

"Cold hands."

He smiled then. "Poor circulation. I have to give you an examination, Gail. And I need to ask you some questions as part of it. Do you feel like answering?"

"Yes." I already felt like a lab specimen with the miraculous gift of speech. I seemed more lucid than I was. This was the moment I'd been waiting for all along. The it's-over moment when everybody comes rushing expertly to my side to . . . do whatever experts do to solve all problems. But I hadn't meant anything like this. Not this Marcus Welby scene. Still, I was calm. Even then maybe I knew I seemed too calm.

A nurse was standing behind Dr. Reynolds. I thought she was Mrs. Danko from *The Rookies*. She never said anything, but Dr. Reynolds was talking. "This is all strictly routine, but it may be a little uncomfortable. Afterward, though, you'll have a good night's sleep."

"At home?"

"No, here. For several days, I expect."

Mrs. Danko, or whoever she was, put my feet into the stirrups at either side of the table and pulled the sheet up until it was a green tent balancing on my knees. She took my hand then, the one without the tube in it. "Now, Gail," Dr. Reynolds said, "you've had a pelvic examination before. Do you know why you're going to have another one now?"

I didn't want to answer, but he waited. "Yes. Because I've . . . been raped."

"This examination is to determine if you've had recent intercourse, and if you've suffered any damage. I'm going to have to insert a speculum." Something metal flashed in his hands. "I've had it in warm water so it's not cold, but you may feel some discomfort, probably more than during the exam I gave you last spring."

He began then, and I understood why the nurse was there beside me. I was clinging to her. Waves of almost-pain began. I tried not to make a sound, though when I tensed and shut my eye tight, my head began to roar and pound. "Okay, Gail, try to relax. I'm going to check your cervical lumen for traces of sperm. The lumen is the entrance to your uterus. I have to take a smear and place it on a slide to look at under the microscope. Now I'm looking at your posterior fornix. That's a small pouch under the entrance of the uterus which I also have to check for secretions and sperm."

After that, I could feel the speculum being removed, and I heard Dr. Reynolds snap on rubber gloves. "Now, Gail, the worst is over. This will be much easier."

Only it wasn't. It didn't take very long though, or didn't seem to. I was numb anyway, wanting to feel nothing. The nurse moved away and dealt with the glass slides. There was the rattling of a metal table on wheels. "There now," Dr. Reynolds said, "you haven't sustained any injuries."

"Haven't I?"

"I mean there was no tearing. Now I want to ask you some questions. They're about your recent medical history. I prescribed birth control pills for you about six months ago, didn't I?"

"Yes."

"When was your last period?"

"It was . . . I'm not too clear about time."

"Yes, I understand."

"It was probably about two weeks ago."

"Was it a normal period for you?"

"Yes."

"And the period before that?"

"They're always the same now that I'm on the pill."

"Do you take your pills regularly?"

"Yes, most of the time."

"Are you sure you've taken the pill every day since your last period?"

"I don't know. I think so."

"Most of the time then?"

"Yes. Mostly out of habit."

"Then you'll be all right. Go on and take the pill until your cycle is complete. I'll see that you get them while you're here in the hospital. You aren't going to get pregnant."

"I want to vomit," I said.

"Nurse." Dr. Reynolds turned around to her, fast.

"No," I said. "I'm not going to. I just want to."

He was standing beside me then, taking my arm in his hands, swabbing it with wet cotton. "I'm going to give you a shot of Valium now, Gail, and then you'll rest."

I didn't feel the needle going in, and usually I can feel it before it hits the skin. I hoped I'd be asleep right away, probably permanently. But time passed while the examining table rocked under me like a rowboat.

Everything got very dull except my hearing. The sound of Dr. Reynolds' voice came very clearly through the screen. He was dictating to the nurse: "Microscopic examinations of vaginal secretions obtained from the posterior fornix indicate numerous motile spermatazoa." Then I heard the word "police." Thinking it was about time for somebody to mention them, I fell away down a dark well, turning as I went.

I opened my eyes again, mad at the Valium for not working. But the glare in the room was from sunlight, and the screens were gone. So was the tube in my hand. It was a hospital room, a very superior one. There was a TV set attached high on the wall, with its screen angled toward the bed. The walls were a restful shade of blue, with framed prints of wild flowers. The bed was very soft, and I thought, *Is this a school day or isn't it?*

There were people in the room, but one of my eyes was plastered shut, and the steel bands that seemed to be running along under the skin of my forehead kept me from looking around. I could only see the man in a chair drawn up close to the bed. And I knew it was the man I'd heard crying before. I focused on him, and he became Dad sitting there.

"You should be at work," I told him, very stern and businesslike. "And look at you. You haven't shaved."

His mouth worked up to a smile, and he said, "But it's Sunday."

"I guess I can accept that excuse just this once." His chin was quivering, and I knew this little word game wasn't working. I tried to think of something that would.

"Are you going to be able to talk to . . . some people?" he said.

"What people?" I didn't think I could cope with anybody else. I just wanted Dad there. When did I ever have him to myself?

"Well, Steve for one. When he hears about you, he'll be battering down the door."

"I guess I don't want to see him yet. Later. Pretty soon. Not now."

"And the police."

"Where are they when you need them?" I asked, trying to fix him with my one eye and make it sparkle. I knew he was crumpling again, and I was trying to put it off, but that was the wrong thing to say. The worst. His eyes were watering, and he was working his hands together, below the level of the bed.

"They were pretty mad because they weren't contacted right away—as soon as Mrs. Montgomery came home last night and . . . found you. It was the hospital that reported the—the crime."

"Are they here now?"

"No. But they'll be here as soon as we let them know you're able to talk."

"Shall we get it over with?" I said, wanting to and not wanting to.

"Whatever you say, sweetheart," he said in a husky whisper.

"No." It was Mother's voice. "Not yet, Neal. She's not ready. I don't want her going through that yet, whatever it is." She walked around the end of the bed. She'd been on my blind side all along. And all I could think of was that I wished she'd go away. I didn't want any interruptions.

But when she was standing beside Dad, wanting to reach out to me, but not doing it, I saw her face. So I knew she'd sat beside me all night. Under her eyes were the brown smudges that she usually erases before breakfast. And her hair wasn't combed.

I started to cry then. It was the three of us, grouped

tight. I wanted Mother there. I never wanted to be out of their sight again. I could see us as three little people, three dots in this huge hateful world, and I cried and cried, and the tears made sounds when they hit the pillow.

Then they were gone. A nurse was there instead, badly blurred, with her needle at the ready. Not the night nurse; a different one. And down the well I went again.

When I woke up the second time, it was almost evening. I was starving for breakfast, lunch, dinner, whatever. But I didn't move because there were people in the room again, and the conversation was about concussion.

Nobody seemed to notice my eye flutter open and close again because Dr. Reynolds was talking. The more medical his monologue, the better I understood it. "We routinely take a culture to check for venereal disease." This was interrupted by a murmur from Mother, not quite a protest. More a moan. "The darkfield exam for syphilis was negative, but we'll have to wait until Tuesday for the gonorrheal culture."

I was struggling up on my elbows then, though my head was cracking apart. "I don't have VD," I said in a loud, clear voice that created sudden silence throughout the room.

"Oh, sweetheart," Mother said, there beside me again, putting her hands out, trying to cover my ears. "Don't listen. We'll take care of . . . it's a necessary procedure . . . they've explained it to—"

"Yes, Mother, but I don't have VD. I mean it's very unlikely."

"But we can't know that, Gail. How could we? It might have been some degenerate who, who—"

"It was a degenerate, Mother, but I'm pretty sure he isn't diseased. Not that way. It was Phil Lawyer."

All the clocks in Oldfield Village skipped a beat. Nobody breathed in the room. Nobody moved. I could see better, propped up on my elbows. And I looked all around with my one good eye at the people looking back. Dr. Reynolds in his white coat, Dad with his hand gripped on the foot of 'my bed. Mrs. Montgomery was farther off with a green glass vase of dahlias from her garden, caught just in the act of setting it down on a table.

Are you sure? Are you sane? The room was suffocating with questions nobody asked. *Concussion can muddle your thinking And shock. You've suffered The Fate Worse Than Death it ruins your life, starting with your brains.*

Mother's hands hovered over me and pulled back. Her lips repeated Phil's name, but without sound. It was Mrs. Montgomery who spoke first. She was still wearing her Saturday night dancing dress, black chiffon, under a polo coat. "Let's not let Steve Pastorini hear that. Not until he has to know."

"Not a word to anybody," Mother said quickly, "until we're sure."

"Phil Lawver raped me. He sent me filthy anonymous notes. He called me on the phone, wherever I was. He spied on Steve and me and followed us. He tortured me for weeks before he picked his time. And then he raped me. It was Phil Lawver. Can you hear me? I'll still be saying it when I don't have concussion and when the stitches are out of my head. It'll still be Phil Lawver."

I was tired again, like I'd delivered a much longer speech. "He'll pay for it," Dad whispered. But even then I wasn't so sure.

They stayed with me in the room while my head got heavier. Mrs. Montgomery fussed with the dahlias, shifting the heads of the blossoms around and around, murmuring conversation to Mother, who wasn't answering. Dad stood at the window with his back to the room, staring out, except that the Venetian blinds were closed. His hands, clasped behind his back, tightened and loosened, like someone giving blood.

The last thing I really heard was Dr. Reynolds saying, "I think you folks better think about getting a lawyer." And then they were gone. When I was alone, I was fully awake for a minute, not more. There was a plaque at the foot of my bed, a bronze square. It was framed by the white mounds of my covered feet. I squinted to read the engraved words.

THE FURNITURE IN THIS ROOM OF OLDFIELD VILLAGE
MEMORIAL HOSPITAL HAS BEEN DONATED THROUGH
THE GENEROSITY OF THE LAWVER FAMILY

Another sign flashed in my mind when I woke up Monday morning. The one on Connie's desk in the city: "Today is the first day of the rest of your life."

Not a promising day. I hurt everywhere, in places where I'd only been numb. There were bruises up high on my legs. I didn't have to look to know. They felt purple and yellow. But my mind was clear, smoldering.

Steve was sitting across the room. He was slumped in a chair. I could see everything that morning without having to concentrate. I watched him before he saw I was awake. Light coming through the blinds striped his face and his rumpled hair. He must have slipped in very early when nobody was looking.

There was time to remember things, like the lunatic moments when I'd suspected even him of . . . being the one. It seemed disloyal and very dumb in the cold light of day. There's such a thing as being too lucid. That was probably the moment when I knew we were really meant to be friends all along, not anything else. Maybe not even close friends. I'd admired him and liked him and we'd played at being lovers, and even that seemed an innocent experiment, and long ago.

"They've got some really weird visiting hours in this place," I said.

He struggled up in the chair, pretending he hadn't been napping. He must have said exactly what he'd been thinking. "In books the hero rescues the girl before anybody can . . . harm her."

"Soap opera," I said. "Not real. How did you know I was here?"

"I went to Mrs. Montgomery's after Dad and I got back from Norwalk, but it was late. The house was dark. I thought you'd gone home, and it was too late to call."

"Mrs. Montgomery had taken me to the hospital."

"I know that now. Your dad called me." We thought our separate thoughts for a few moments. I knew Dad hadn't told him everything, not that it was Phil.

"I wasn't there when you needed me," Steve said.

"It would have happened, sometime, someplace." I could see that confused him. "At least you were with your dad— and out of town. Nobody can make you take the rap." I was making perfect sense, and he was wondering if I was talking out of my head. I was, partly. My mind was floating somewhere above my body.

"Do you feel all right?"

"Damaged. Maybe not beyond repair. I don't know. I think I'm still tranquilized."

"Can you . . . put it behind you?"

"Forget? Pretend it didn't happen? No. That's what my parents are going to want me to do. I can tell. I made too many mistakes before. I'd better learn from them. Anyway, I couldn't forget if I wanted to. I have to talk to the police and probably a lawyer."

His glasses threw flashes of sunlight when he pulled them off and rubbed his temples. Still he didn't think to come over to the bed, and I didn't expect him to. "How did the . . . attacker get in the house?"

"I let him in. I thought it was . . . I thought it was Mrs. Montgomery coming home."

"No, you thought it was me, didn't you? It was too early for Mrs. Montgomery, wasn't it?" He looked like a little boy, and I wanted to spare him. But I settled for the truth.

"Yes, I was hoping it was you. Let's not blame ourselves. We're not the culprits."

"Can you identify . . . him?"

"Yes."

"Then whatever you have to go through with the police is worth it."

"Maybe."

"What can I do? Tell me something. I feel—useless. Worse than useless. I know what my dad would do. He'd go down to the VFW and get up a posse to rid the county of perverts."

"My particular pervert would slip through their net. Just stay here and don't say anything. This is going to be a long day. It's important to me to start it with a friend."

"Is that what we are now—friends?"

"Don't sell friendship short. It's too rare." We didn't say any more until the rattle of the breakfast carts echoed along the hall. "Go on to school," I said then. "Don't cut. They'll only throw you out of here in a minute or so."

He lingered in the doorway until I wanted to scream. "Shall I . . . do you want this kept quiet?"

"It probably couldn't be. It probably shouldn't be. But yes, keep it quiet if you can."

"Maybe nobody'll have to know," he said. "Except what about Alison? She'll wonder where you are. What'll I tell her?"

"Alison? Oh Lord!" I said. "I'd forgotten about Alison. Go on, Steve, get moving—quick!" He gave me another bewildered look and was gone. The door just closed behind him before I began to laugh in terrible, tinny peals. I laughed until I was crying into a knot I made out of the pillow. I had hysterics all by myself and didn't even try to stop. And they were triggered by Alison, of all people. Yes. Whatever will we tell Alison?

The day nurse was tight-lipped and looked me over like something in a jar at the Harvard medical school. She bristled and bustled. And I wondered if she disapproved of all patients or just rape cases. She combed my hair, washed my face around the swollen stitched part, and refused to let me have a mirror. But she gave me two breakfasts. I might have gotten a third one out of her except that the door opened, and there stood a man who could only be the police chief.

I think I'd seen him drifting around the village in the police cruiser with the brace of red lights clamped on the roof. He was big-bellied and bullnecked and looked his part. The room was instantly heavy with dead cigar smoke. There was another policeman behind him, an apple-cheeked kid standing in the big man's shadow. They were both armed to the teeth. At least they had guns in holster belts. And that seems overdressed for a hospital call.

"Hold it right where you stand!" the nurse barked. She could have wrestled both of them to the floor. "Doctor say you could come in here?"

"You can cut on out," the chief said, not quite meeting her eye. "We got a report on this the night before last. Been hampered in our investigation long enough—too long. We got to get us some information out of this girl, if she's the one who says—"

"You're not talking to this girl alone, mister," the nurse snapped.

"*Officer* to you, lady."

"*Nurse* to you, buddy!"

"Okay, okay." The officer hitched up his belt and tried to stake out territory in the doorway. "What are you, one of them women's libbers? You can stay in the room with her if you want to make this your business."

"It's my business to see my patients aren't hassled. And that's big business around this place. You talk to this girl when the doctor says so and when her parents say so. Until then—out!"

I was almost as afraid of her as the police chief was, once we were alone again. She jerked hospital corners in my bed sheets until I felt bound like a mummy. Still she said nothing. After a quick look around the room, she marched out.

I was lying there thinking what a poor place a hospital is for peace and quiet when the door opened very slowly and the police chief and his partner were standing there. They were looking for the nurse, and when they didn't see her, the chief swaggered in. He snapped his fingers, and the young kid took out a note pad and a ballpoint.

"Okay, honey, we want to get on top of this matter. A couple of questions."

"I don't think . . . maybe Dr. Reynolds ought to be here."

"He's making his rounds about now," the chief said. "He'll be along before we're finished, most likely."

"My parents—"

"Little early for visiting hours. What's the matter, honey, don't you want to cooperate?"

Is there an answer to that when two hundred pounds of the law is leaning over your bed? I started a long version of the story, hoping somebody would come in pretty soon. The story took longer than I'd planned, with his questions breaking in. "You baby-sit for this Mrs. Montgomery regular?"

"Yes, every Saturday night."

"What's a good-looking kid like you baby-sitting for Saturday nights? Haven't you got a boyfriend?"

"Yes, but . . ."

"But what?"

"But what's that got to do with anything?" The young cop was forgetting to take notes. He kept looking back and forth at the two of us.

"Your boyfriend ever come over and keep you company when you're baby-sitting?"

"No."

"Well, go on. Tell it like it was, just in your own words. I'm all ears."

"I'd called St . . . my boyfriend, and his mother answered so I asked her to have him come over when he got home because—"

"Because you were feeling kind of lonesome, right?"

"Because I was feeling scared."

"Scared of what, the dark?"

"I'd been getting phone calls, notes. I was scared because a boy was trying to scare me."

"You're kind of grown up to let a thing like that worry you, aren't you?"

"No, I don't think anybody is."

"So somebody comes to the door, and you let him in, and he pulls a gun on you, right?"

"No. I mean I let him in, but he didn't have a gun."

"A knife, maybe."

"No."

"Now wait a minute, honey. Let me get this straight in my mind. You open the door to a perfect stranger and without threatening you, he rapes you, right?"

I could feel a thickness in my throat. It was the panic I'd felt when Phil Lawver started walking toward me. That same no-place-to-hide feeling. "No, that's not right. He *wasn't* a stranger. I let him in because I know him and he overpowered me, threw me down, and then knocked me out with the fireplace poker."

"Oh yeah." He squinted at my forehead. "You got some stitches up there. How'd it happen?"

"I just told you."

"Okay, honey. I think I got the drift of it now." He rubbed the back of his big neck and took a deep breath. I barely sensed that he was playing his role for the benefit of the younger cop. "Let me run it back for you. A friend of yours—I'm not saying it's your boyfriend—a good-looking kid like you knows plenty of boys. Anyway, this particular one drops by where you're baby-sitting. He knows you're there because you sit regular. And you and him talk on the phone—keep in touch.

"It's just the two of you together. The little kids are asleep upstairs. There's nothing much on TV. You start horsing around a little, completely innocent. All you kids do it. Then you lead him on a little, and he gets—overheated. Tries to get you to do what you don't want to do. Or let's be honest about it. He gets you to do what you both want to do, but you're a nice girl and don't give in that easy.

"So maybe there's some rough stuff. The two of you tussle around a little, and you bump your head. So here you've got you this nasty cut on the head and how are you going to explain that to your folks? So you kind of build up a story around it. That about the way things went?"

My head began to pound again. And somehow I managed to do the only possible right thing. I reached over to the little bulb-shaped thing with the button in it to ring for the nurse. The chief saw me just before I could touch it.

"Hold on there, honey. Maybe I got it wrong. Maybe we'd better take it from the top." He stood there, with a great show of patience while I tried to tell the whole thing again. The only way I could get through it was by fastening my eyes on the young cop who hadn't said anything and looked uncomfortable. I got right to the end that time, and then the chief said, "Okay now, honey, so be it. Let's have the name of this boy."

"Phil Lawver." The young cop seemed to come alive and scrawled the name on his pad.

The chief turned on him and roared, "That's a helluva time to start taking notes! Scratch that!" He turned back to me and leaned over the bed. I could smell bacon on his breath. "You trying to involve the Lawver boy. Otis Lawver's son?"

"He raped me."

The chief looked very weary then, and disgusted. "Honey, you're just asking for trouble. You know that?"

CHAPTER

Eleven

There was screaming that echoed down the hospital halls, metallic echoes bouncing off all the flat, smooth, polished surfaces. My screaming. All I had to do was ring for the nurse, but I screamed instead, loud howls, finally forming words. *"Get . . . them . . . out . . . of . . . here!"* The screams hurt my own ears and wouldn't stop.

The next moment the room was busy with people. The nurse was across the room on squeaky shoes, booming in the chief's ear at the top of her big lungs. Dr. Reynolds was right behind her. My screams slid into blubbering hiccups. The chief kept clearing his throat. "She was cool as a cucumber up to just a little bit ago. She's a little mixed up though. Maybe it'd be better if we come on back a little later on."

They were gone then, and Dr. Reynolds was beside me, pretending to examine my stitches, trying to swing us both back into the doctor-patient routine. "Don't give me another shot of Valium or anything. I'll be all right in a minute."

"I won't," he said and stood there holding my hand while I tried to stop shuddering and sobbing.

Down at the foot of the bed, the nurse was shaking out a blanket. She was deep purple and muttering something about a "tin-badge creep" and a few other words.

Dr. Reynolds gave her an uncertain glance, but I whispered, "That's my guardian angel down there." She muttered on, but I think she heard me.

"Gail, did you tell the police it was Phil Lawver?" Dr. Reynolds asked.

"Yes."

"Then I guess you won't be bothered by the chief again."

"Why?"

"You just won't."

"But why?"

"Because he's not going to get involved with an arrest."

"The Lawvers are above that, aren't they?" I think I'd known that for as long as I'd been conscious.

"It's not that simple." But he wasn't looking my way when he spoke. "You can get up and sit on the edge of the bed." I didn't want to. I didn't want to take one step nearer the world.

The rest of the morning got no better. I was down from my Valium high, and the screaming had clarified the bleakness of the day. When Mother arrived and heard what happened, she told Dr. Reynolds in very direct terms that "our own doctor wouldn't have called in the police." He escaped then, to his pregnant patients, probably relieved for a change of scene.

Dad came shortly after that, with our attorney. Mrs. Montgomery was back too, standing around in the background, never taking off her coat, looking haunted.

Finally it got through to me that she felt the whole business was her fault. When she was beside my bed, I said, "Look, it was going to happen. If not at your house, some other place." (Hadn't I said this all before, to Steve? How many people was I going to have to reassure?) "I should have—"

"You shouldn't have had to do anything, Gail," she said. "You have a right to . . . to be safe. And I knew you were worried and jumpy. I've gone over it a hundred times in my mind. I should have foreseen . . . I'm sick about what happened to you, and yet I keep thinking about my own kids, growing up in this town, growing up anywhere. I'm scared for them, and I want to make this up to you, and— and I can't do anything for anybody."

"But you care," I said. "That counts." I had to say something.

She cried then, and it upset me because I thought of her as a very tough lady.

Dad approached me with caution, fumbling for my hand. "We're going to try to get some . . . satisfaction out of this, if that's the word." The lawyer stepped up beside him. "This is Ted Naylor. He's talked to Dr. Reynolds, and he's more or less in the picture already."

Mr. Naylor was young and wore a three-piece suit. I noticed he was good-looking, though my interest in the opposite sex was at a very low ebb. Permanently low, I thought. He sat down next to the bed, and Mother and Dad crouched on the edges of chairs farther off. Mrs. Montgomery didn't know whether to stay or leave, but Mother beckoned her back from the door. I was glad she wanted her there.

"I understand the police have given you a hard time, Gail," Mr. Naylor said. I nodded.

"Before we get into anything else, why don't you tell me what you think the police chief's attitude was."

It wasn't hard to put into words. "He thought it wasn't a . . . rape at all. He thought maybe I was . . . involved with Phil Lawver and trying to get him into trouble because I was—mad at him or feeling guilty or something."

"That's the usual official posture," Mr. Naylor said. "And if he hadn't had the medical report, he'd have been convinced nothing happened at all."

"Is the medical report a point in our favor?"

"It would be if . . ."

"If what?"

"Several ifs. If the assailant had forced his way in—picked a lock or broken a window.

"If he'd been a stranger.

"If you'd been a virgin.

"If you hadn't been on birth control pills, because that's part of the medical report.

"Even, I'm sorry to say, if you'd been screaming and hysterical and incoherent throughout the police interview. And . . ."

"And if it hadn't been Phil Lawver," I said.

"Yes, if it hadn't been Phil Lawver. That may seem the biggest *if* in our minds, Gail. But the combination of the other factors would work against you anyway, even in the unlikely event that we could take this to court."

"What's so damned unlikely about that, Ted?" Dad said. He was on his feet, pacing around, ready to punch a wall. Maybe ready to punch Mr. Naylor.

"Sit down, Neal. I can't offer you a thing you'll want to hear. But I can give you a pretty accurate projection of the way things work. First of all, our next step should logically be to swear out a complaint against the Lawver boy. We can do this even without the cooperation of the police. But the court can deny our complaint. Moreover, if we succeeded in getting an arrest, there's the problem of a countersuit. The Lawyers could get us for false arrest. There weren't any witnesses, for a start."

Mrs. Montgomery burst out, "But I—"

"You were there later, Mrs. Montgomery. I mean actual on-the-spot witnesses." She crumpled back in her chair.

"Now then, let's proceed on the long shot that we managed to get an arrest. The judge may opt against prosecution entirely. In most cases, typical cases, he'll let the rape charge go if the rapist agrees to plead guilty to a lesser charge: assault, disorderly conduct—any one of a dozen completely irrelevant charges. This is called plea-bargaining, and it's arranged entirely between the court authority and the defense lawyer. I—we have absolutely no control over it.

"However if we did, by some miracle, bring this to trial, you'd get a public grilling, Gail, a good deal more savage than the chief of police is capable of dealing out. You'd be questioned under oath. If you admitted to having had any sexual relationship with any boy at any previous time, the proceedings are over, and we've lost.

"But that key question might come many hours after a lot of other questions, all designed to implicate you as a willing partner. To portray you as provocative, immoral, even delinquent. The defending lawyer doesn't even have to accuse you of anything directly. He can imply."

"We can't have that," Mother murmured.

"But what about Phil?" I said.

"Phil," Mr. Naylor said heavily, "would be portrayed as a star athlete, a handsome, gifted, promising boy from one of the best families, whose entire future is jeopardized by a scheming, possibly unbalanced young girl out to ruin him because of some obscure grudge of her own."

"Ted, I can't take any more of this!" Dad shouted. "What good—"

"What good am I as your lawyer? Not much, I guess, if you think I can revolutionize the entire legal setup—at the expense of your daughter. I'll go with this as far as you want me to go, as far as Gail wants. But I wouldn't be fair if I didn't tell you what we're up against."

"But Phil's crazy," I said. "Who knows what he'll do next? Those letters just show—"

"What letters?" Mr. Naylor said.

"Two of them. Even the guidance counselor said one of them was psychotic. They weren't signed, but Phil sent them. He admitted it."

"Where are they?"

I had to stop and think. "Alison. She has one. I mean she had it."

"Oh no," Mother said.

"Who's Alison?"

"She's a friend—a girl I know. But that's not the point. She and Phil Lawver—"

"Say no more. What about the other letter?" Mr. Naylor said.

"Mr. Sampson. He's the Dean of Boys at school. He took it."

"You'd gone with this problem to him—before?"

"Yes. But even at the time I knew he didn't take it seriously. Probably didn't even keep the note. And if he found out . . . well, if he had an incriminating letter that could be traced to Phil, he'd destroy it even if he hasn't already."

"Don't sell him short, Gail," Mr. Naylor said. "He might be able—"

"He got where he is by being appointed by the Lawvers."

"This is why people take the law into their own hands," Dad said in a quavering voice.

"Don't be one of those people, Neal," Mr. Naylor said. "The situation's grim enough. In any case, a couple of anonymous letters wouldn't turn the tide." He stood up then, and I thought he was finished with us. But he said to Mother and Dad, "Do you think I might have a few minutes' conversation with Gail alone? No secret deals. Believe me, we aren't in a position to make any. But I'd like to talk to her quietly if you'll permit it."

I'll never forget the defeated looks on their faces—Mrs. Montgomery's too. I asked Mother to hand me my robe. It was time to get out of that bed.

When they went out into the hall, I sat on the edge of the bed, picking at the fuzz on my robe to keep my hands busy. *Now I know why people smoke*, I thought. Still, there was less tension in the room.

"I'm more a bearer of bad news than a lawyer, in your dad's opinion.

"And I don't have any more legal options to explore with you, Gail. There are some other considerations, though. Do you feel up to them?"

"I don't know. I'm getting past the stunned stage, beginning to worry about other people. That's why you asked my parents to leave, isn't it?"

"Yes. After all, you're the injured party, however the law would look upon you. Even if you decided against telling me to try for an arrest, that doesn't wrap things up. You're going to have to be very strong. You're going to have to live in a town where Phil Lawver is walking around free. You're going to have to put up with the attitudes of other people—including the people who love you. And however positive your outlook, you're going to face a lot of changes, in other people and yourself. You only think now you're getting past the stunned stage."

"The worst is yet to come?"

"Believe it or not, yes. I said you're going to have to be strong. That involves confronting the past before you look ahead."

"What does that mean?"

"Knowing that no matter what anybody else thinks, you did nothing to deserve this. There are plenty of people who think like the police chief, that there is no such thing as rape.

"I don't have you on the witness stand, so don't answer out loud what I'm about to ask you. Answer to yourself. Apart from going to the counselor at school, why didn't you tell other people you were being threatened?"

"I—"

"No, don't tell me. Tell yourself."

It was like running a film in reverse. The events skipped back in a blur, jumbling up. Alison saying, "It never happened, Gail." My mother saying, "What has that Steve Pastorini done to you?" Connie saying, "Men can't afford to fail. It's like bred into them." It seemed that everybody had turned blind eyes and deaf ears to me.

But that wasn't quite right. I'd sealed myself off from them too. Why? Embarrassment? Panic? That stupid, babyish feeling left over from childhood that, no matter what, nothing this bad could really be happening to me?

"It's too much to sort out at once," I said to Mr. Naylor.

"I know," he said. "But you've begun. Don't try to carry the weight of the world on your shoulders from now on. And don't pretend everything's fine when it isn't.

"Yell bloody murder if anybody does or says anything you don't like. There are many ways of being assaulted apart from what you've already been through—and that includes the police chief as well as Phil.

"On the other hand, you can't go around making accusations you can't prove. You'll be walking a tightrope, no matter what. Am I overburdening you with advice?"

"No, I don't believe so. I've got to start thinking."

"Good. That's enough for now. I'm going to talk to your mother and father. I'll tell them that you're going to have to make most of your own decisions. Maybe they'll understand, maybe not. We'll see. You'll see."

"Did you know my dad's out of work?"

"Yes. But I didn't know you did. Why bring that up?"

"Because it makes everything harder for him, I suppose. He probably thinks he was so bogged down by his own problems that he couldn't see . . . anything else. Will you do something for me? When you talk to him, tell him I know about his losing his job. That even though I was worried about it, I couldn't do anything to help him. There's a kind of parallel there."

Mr. Naylor looked at me a moment, gave me an appraising look. "I think you're going to manage to get through this, Gail." Then very abruptly he said, "Do I try for an arrest or not? I'll do what you say. And I'll do my best to convince your family that they should abide by your decision."

"I don't want to be raped again—in a courtroom. I don't want to go through that without a hope of getting satisfaction."

"*Satisfaction* was your father's word. Think about what *you* want first of all. Just because I painted a dark picture of what would happen, I don't want to sway you too much.

I'm not exactly Don Quixote, but I'm willing to tilt with a windmill or two if so directed by my client."

"Meaning?"

"Meaning I'll fight a lost cause if you say so."

"No. Because if we lose, the Lawvers win."

"Then that's about it. But remember, they win anyway."

"There's just one more thing you can tell me," I said. "Why does the law protect the rapist instead of the victim?"

"Because the law is wrong."

CHAPTER

Twelve

"Planning to put bars on that window?" I asked Dad. While I thrashed around in my own bed, he spent hours taking out the screens and putting in the storm windows. He'd given up going in to New York every day, and I guess winterizing the house was an ideal way for him to patrol the place. He worked in slow motion at the top of a ladder, wearing a boyish navy-surplus knit cap on the back of his head. "And listen, Dad, *soldiers* with mild concussion get up in about two hours and go back to the war. It happens on *M*A*S*H* all the time. The doctor wouldn't have let me come home if he thought I had to be bedfast."

"Don't cite *M*A*S*H* to me," he said, peering in the window. "I was in the real Korean War. Anyway, it's only been a few days, and besides—"

"Besides, you want me where you can keep an eye on me."

"I guess so," he said, pretending to keep busy. "And what's the hurry? Those stitches won't be coming out for another ten days, at the earliest. You can't go back to—go any place looking like that." He closed the conversation by hammering in a storm window, and then lingered a little longer, looking at me, making a funny face, before his head disappeared below the sill.

None of us had mentioned my going back to school yet. It seemed like a cold July instead of November. The stitches did look like railroad tracks running into my eyebrow. They turned my stomach whenever I looked in the mirror, which was too often. Mother limited her side of conversations strictly to concussion and scarless stitches. Rape wasn't mentioned in the sanctuary of my room. Neither was the future. But every night I heard the mutter of talk downstairs between Mother and Dad, far into the night.

"If by some chance I *did* get pregnant because of this," I'd said to Mother in a low moment, "I'd have an abortion."

"Don't talk like that," she said.

"I would. I'd be a very peculiar mother because I'm never going to have anything to do with men for the rest of my life."

"Don't . . ."

"You said to me once that if I had everything now, what would I have to look forward to. Well, I've *had* IT!"

"Don't, don't talk like that," she said, sounding strangled.

The florist delivered a huge foil-covered pot of yellow chrysanthemums on the day after I came home. They were like sunshine, overpowering Mrs. Montgomery's drooping dahlias that came home from the hospital with me.

Flowers—from the best florist in town. They were like a

signal sent from the outside world. Mother looked worried. But the doorbell rang again just as she set them down, and she dashed out again. She was at her best when she could keep busy, when she was darting from task to task with her skirt snapping around her legs.

An envelope peeked out of the satin bow around the flower pot. I ripped it open, wondering. Inside, a florist's card with a signature: PHIL LAWVER

My head whirled while down below Mother admitted a visitor. I was deaf to the conversation as they climbed the stairs. When the door opened, I slipped the card under the sheet and wished for Valium.

At that moment nothing much would have astounded me. But I could hardly believe it when Madam Malevich strode into the room. Mother followed, popeyed. This was as close as she'd ever come to the living legend. She could have kept anybody else out.

"So, you live! The rumors conflict on that point, so Malevich must know for herself!" She stood in the middle of the room, filling it up. An enormous handbag dangled from one large elbow. She was wearing bright purple wool drapings, and her hair was newly blackened.

I was sure I never wanted to see anybody for the rest of my life. But Madam Malevich was the exception to all rules.

"You are asking yourself," she boomed at me, "what Malevich does outside the walls of the school one hour before closing time. The answer is that she comes and she goes as she pleases. No, no, I do not play the truant officer, only the truant. But the rumors grow like a great whirlwind, and idle tittle-tattle tires me."

"Oh dear," Mother murmured, "how does word get around so quickly?"

"Ah, young minds wiz too little to occupy their cranial capacities. And a school is a small village within another small village. And the young who are never told to be quiet therefore never are.

"Moreover, there are doctors in this town who talk of hospital business at their dinner tables, and these doctors also have children."

"Valerie Cathcart," I said.

"And if not she, someone else," Madam Malevich said, dismissing a whole cloud of Valerie Cathcarts. "You are looking well though wounded," she observed, skewering me with a look.

"What are they saying?" Mother asked faintly.

"Saying? Saying?" Lowered into the only chair in my room, Madam Malevich glanced up at Mother. "They say that Gail was set upon by a gang of dope fiends and thrashed to within an inch of her life. That she lay on the operating table between this world and the next for countless hours. That she will not walk again. That only a machine keeps her alive. That housebreakers intent upon robbing a woman named Montgomery overpowered Gail as she protected this woman's young ones. That Gail and the boy who is her special friend—that Pastorini boy—I don't know him, for he's not my student—that she and he were involved in an automobile mishap and that he alone escaped uninjured. The Pastorini boy is silent as a clam, and this only fans the winds of speculation. They speak too of rape—"

"Can I get you something, Mrs. Malevich?" Mother broke in quickly.

"I can make no claim to the title Mrs., but a nice cup of tea wiz lemon would be welcome," she said calmly. Then Mother realized she'd made just the wrong move and that

126

she'd have to leave the two of us alone. She wavered as long as she could, but Malevich waited her out.

Madam Malevich was the last person in my life I'd have thought of confiding in. And maybe if it hadn't been for that florist's card lying hidden in my bed, I'd have stalled her. Though I don't know how.

"I am a busy person," she said unexpectedly. "No. That is not the correct term. I am a busy*body*. It is true. My friends are gone—who knows where? I have little in common wiz the people in this town. So I make the business of others my own. But also, I care for my students. If I did not, their laughter would anger me. And the world does not need one more bitter old woman. I come here now, for I am concerned about you. Not everyone could have got past your mother who in her kindness seeks to shield you. She would do better to throw open the doors of her house and invite in those who indulge in morbid gossip that puts you at death's door. But I do not mean to criticize her. Young girls are critical enough of their mothers.

"In any case, you will not grip the public imagination long. Their attention span is too short. Poof!" she said, waving two fingers in the air. "They soon forget."

"I was raped," I said, looking directly into her black eyes.

"Ah, so I feared. There is always that nugget of truth in all talk. I was ravished myself many times, in those primitive films I made. You saw one yourself. The old, old stories of the maiden who resists man's desire and her own, only to be liberated by what she cannot forestall. Harmless myths, I thought when I was young and dazed with dreaming. But not harmless when the myth fixes itself into a sick mind. Who did this to you?"

I never hesitated: "Phil Lawver."

"You can't go around making accusations you can't prove," the lawyer had said. But being in the same room with Madam Malevich was very different from being in the same room with Mr. Naylor.

"So," she said. "It is not entirely unexpected." Anybody else would at least have gasped. "I knew the Lawvers before you were born. They have always lived too much . . . as if they were the only people on the earth. It does not astonish me that in time they produce a child who cannot live in a world wiz others."

"But he will," I said. "He won't be punished for this."

"Before you are as old as I," she replied, nearly sighing, "you will cease looking for justice at every turn."

Mother was suddenly at the door, holding a tea tray. "You told?" she said to me, horrified.

"Yes, she told." Madam Malevich lifted herself out of the chair. "Unspoken truths only fester. But I repeat nothing. My words cannot do or undo. Who listens? I will go now, Mrs. Osburne. This is not, after all, the occasion for a tea party."

She shuffled across the room, looking older, I thought, than when she'd come. But she hesitated at the door, and she wasn't a woman who hesitated. "I say my words are useless," she said, looking back at me. "But though you are young, you know already you cannot run from this thing. I will send to you someone who cannot run from it either. That much I can do, and no more." Then she was gone, waving a hand behind her round back that told Mother not to see her out.

When we heard the front door click behind her, Mother said, "She's a little eccentric, isn't she?"

"Not very," I said.

"Did she send the flowers?"

"I guess she must have."

"Who does she think she's going to send to see you? Because I don't want a lot of people trailing in here and—"

"Who knows?" I said. But I knew who she'd send.

Madam Malevich's visit didn't crumble Mother's defenses. No one else got past the front-door barrier until the end of the week. Steve came as far as the front steps every day, but he handed over my books and assignments to Mother.

I spent one long afternoon with the sun flooding in across those terrible chrysanthemums, wondering if Steve and I could start over, fresh. Wondering if . . . being with him would only be using him. He'd be sympathetic and very gentle. But then I decided you can't use people for your own personal therapy. Unless of course, you're Phil Lawver.

Madam Malevich sent Alison. Maybe Mother knew that when she let her in. Anyway, she left us alone. It was Friday afternoon, and school had been over for hours. I didn't turn on a light. Alison lurked at the door. "Hi. Where've you been?" she said.

"Where've *you* been?"

"I'd have come sooner, but . . ."

She'd brought me a box of chocolate truffles and approached the bed on my bad side, the one with the railroad tracks. The room was dim though, and she didn't look right at me. I'd been in and out of bed since Wednesday, but I was lying down when she came. It made me feel stagey.

"I can't stay," she said, perching on the chair, but not taking off her coat. "How are you feeling? Everyone wondered. You know how Valerie Cathcart runs off at the mouth."

"She may be right for all I know." I let the silence last.

With the storm windows in, the room seemed sealed like a jar. I guess I wanted Alison to squirm. She was trying not to and giving me her serene profile.

"Well, what happened?" she finally said, very impatient. I flicked on the bedside lamp. The skin around the stitches was still puffy and inflamed—how well I knew. Black X's on a red field. She looked once and fixed her eyes on the far corner of the room.

"I tripped at the top of the stairs, fell all the way down, and was raped while passing the landing."

"Is that supposed to be funny?" Alison said, retreating.

"You know what happened, Alison. Did he tell you?"

"Steve hasn't said a word. You know how he is when he gets into one of those moods of his."

"I'm not talking about Steve, and you know it. It was Phil. He was the one who sent me those notes. You knew it from the first. You probably recognized his handwriting. You probably—"

"Why, you dirty little liar," Alison whispered. If she'd really been surprised, she'd have bellowed at the top of her voice. "What are you trying to pull?"

More silence.

"You got yourself into . . . some kind of trouble, probably with *Steve*. And this is your way of getting out of it *and* hurting Phil. I always knew you were jealous of—us. What'd you ever have going for yourself except with that dip, Steve? You were going *nowhere*, Gail. And now you think you can . . . why Phil doesn't know you're alive!"

"He didn't when he left me unconscious on the floor."

"You really have gotten yourself into a mess, haven't you?"

"I'll get out of it, Alison. Will you?"

"You're out of your mind. What are you babbling about?"

130

"I'm not much in the mood for offering friendly advice. But Phil's through with me now. Is he through with you?"

"Are you kidding? This doesn't make any difference to —I mean what does this have to do with Phil and me?"

While I waited her out, I sensed that someone was standing on the other side of my bedroom door. It figured. Mother wasn't about to let Alison in without hearing for herself. I didn't mind. I was learning the necessity of witnesses.

"I think you'd better be careful about Phil," I said, quietly but clearly.

"*You're* the one who'd better be careful, Gail, throwing around accusations. If Phil ever thought . . . why he doesn't even notice you're not in school."

"Yes he does, Alison. He sent me these flowers." I didn't like that being heard on the other side of the door, but it needed to be said.

"I think when you hit your head, something happened to your mind," Alison said, almost kindly.

I rummaged around in the table drawer, pulling out the florist's card hidden there. "Here's a note you won't tear up, Alison. The only one Phil signed." I held it up to her until she looked at it. He'd written his name in oversized letters. She laced up her fingers in her lap, knowing she couldn't grab for it.

"Well, that just proves . . . he didn't have anything to do with . . . anything. Who in their right mind would . . . rape somebody and then send her flowers. It's crazy."

"That's what I'm trying to say to you, Alison. I think you'd better be careful. I doubt if Phil understands that he did anything wrong—or could do anything wrong. I guess that's what the flowers mean."

"If anybody has amnesia, it's you, Gail." Alison tucked her hair behind her ears. "I'm not listening to any more of this. I know Phil. And he's certainly no *rapist*. If anything, he's—"

"He's what?"

"He's too much of a gentleman."

"He's a very disturbed gentleman," I said. "For my sake I'd like to see him in jail. For his sake I'd like to see him in a mental institution."

"And what about *me*?" Alison yelled, jumping up. "Have you got room in your paranoid little fantasy for *me*?"

"For your sake, Alison, I wish Phil hadn't been born rich and handsome and social. Then you could have gone after somebody safer."

"Okay, that's enough. I've had it," she said, jerking a knot in her belt. *"But listen to this and remember it.* If you ever have the nerve to show your face at school again, and if you *ever* try to spoil anything for Phil and me, I'll go straight to Mrs. Lawver and tell her. And the Lawvers will run you and your nothing family out of this town."

"I wish we were already gone," I said, mostly to myself.

"So do I!" Alison screamed. She rushed to the door and banged it back against the wall, pushing past somebody who was standing out there in the hall. But it wasn't Mother. It was Dad.

CHAPTER

Thirteen

"I wrote a letter to Aunt Viola," Mother said on Sunday evening. "Aunt Viola in Harrisburg." She stood there, fingering the wooden curlicues on the foot of my bed.

Aunt Viola. Mother's aunt, not mine. Aunt Viola who started me out at birth with the add-a-pearl necklace. Who kept sending me educational toys right up through my thirteenth birthday. Aunt Viola of the annual twenty-dollar Christmas check.

"She's—you know she has more money than she knows what to do with."

Aunt Viola and money. What's behind this? I wondered. Mother had spent the week weighing every word she spoke. Now the words were catching in her throat. She was so intent on her thoughts that she only cast a troubled glance at me. I was lying fully dressed on top of my made-up bed, when Mother still wanted to see me in pajamas between the sheets.

The chrysanthemums had vanished from my bedside

once when I was out of the room. I'd come back. They were gone.

"I always could be absolutely frank with Aunt Viola," Mother said. "She always understood. Anything."

"You wrote her about me?"

"Yes."

"Why?"

"Because I thought, because I knew she'd be willing to help."

"How could she?"

"It's nothing definite. But I thought, under the circumstances, she'd be willing to pay your tuition. If you wanted to go away to school. Not this semester, of course. I don't want you even *thinking* about school right now. But after the winter break. You could certainly get into a very nice boarding school for your last year and a half and—"

"Oh Mother." What could I say? I'd spent all day long on a plan of my own, working up my courage. Now this. And she was racking her brains to help. I couldn't even let myself get mad at her. "Mother, is this the kind of thing you and Dad talk about at night, late?"

"Oh no, nothing like that. Don't say a word to him about this until we hear—"

"I won't, Mother. I won't breathe a word to him about it. Because I'm not going away to school. Even Madam Malevich said I couldn't run from this."

"Oh that funny old lady. Do you realize how often I've heard you laugh about her?"

"I guess I was laughing only because the rest did. And do you know what people say about girls who suddenly disappear to boarding schools in the middle of the year?"

"You wouldn't be around to hear whatever they say. I'm trying my best to think of a plan—"

"So am I—"

"—that we can all live with."

"Dad couldn't live with that plan."

"If you knew, Gail, what this is doing to him. I promised myself I wouldn't say anything like that to you, and here I am blurting it out. But if you knew what he's going through. He was so *certain* something could be done legally, and now he's just—floundering. He'd be delighted to see you have a—fresh start."

"But he couldn't afford my tuition and board bills if I went away. How do you think he'd feel if I was Aunt Viola's charity case?"

She stood at the foot of my bed with her arms wrapped around her middle. I could almost see her pity turning back on herself. "I suppose you'd both fight me on any idea I came up with," she said quietly.

"Don't send the letter to Aunt Viola, Mother."

The walls of my room began creeping toward me. The bulletin board loomed. The mirror reflected railroad tracks at every turn. The gray ring on the table where the chrysanthemum pot had been. Initiating my plan, I kept consulting the closet, pulling dresser drawers out too far until they tipped. Taking the first steps.

I went downstairs for dinner before they had a chance to bring it up. No more meals on trays. Mother and Dad were both in the kitchen. When they saw me, they stepped apart like a pair of guilty teen-agers. Cut-off words hung over the sink. Dinner was nowhere. Mother's hand slipped off the arm of Dad's coat. He had a death grip on the car keys.

You could have cut the atmosphere with a knife. Dad was going someplace. Mother wasn't. Where?

"Why aren't you in bed?" they asked, coming together in chorus.

"Where are you going?" I looked right at Dad. His face was colorless. *Stop looking so middle-aged.* He seemed to be somebody who'd just missed the last train and was willing to run for it.

"He's not going *anyplace*," Mother said, but not to me.

"I'm going over to the Lawvers, Gail."

Could I picture that? The Volvo in the circular drive. Dad's hand on the knocker. Phil himself answering the door. Or, no—maybe Edna. He'd probably get in. And then the frosty, mildly astonished reception. The voices on both sides determined to be low, civilized. The disbelief, the there-must-be-some-mistake. The blank look of remote astonishment on Phil's face. Veiled threats. Ice forming on the chandeliers. Dad's accumulated anger boiling over. All his angers. The mention of lawyers, but not by him. Lawver lawyers. The we-think-you'd-better-leave. I couldn't picture it—not the conclusion.

"It won't work," I said. "They always entertain on Sunday nights. Their set—the Hathaways, the Bradfords, the Wycoffs, sometimes the Forresters. They wouldn't be alone." I was pulling names out of a hat, guessing.

"See?" Mother said, gripping his arm again. "You'd only make a fool of—you can't touch them. Nobody can."

"I'll end up lying under a bush somewhere," Dad said, "waiting for a chance to kill that kid." The car keys rattled down on the counter.

We huddled together that night, brought the Sony into the dining room and watched everything on it. From family hour right through to Kojak and Bronk. We saw crimes being solved all evening. That night I dreamed of having brothers, battalions of them. And of Dad and me on a Ferris wheel. Analyze that. I didn't have the time. The next morning I went to school.

I'd laid out my clothes the night before. Even had a dress rehearsal. I experimented with makeup above my eye. Too heavy in the daylight. So I painfully wiped and picked off crusty tan pancake around the places where the stitches pulled at the skin. All my cosmetics were tough and cracked in their tubes, ancient relics of the days when Alison and I practiced "makeup hints." The bruises on my legs were faded. I could even take gym if I wanted to. The dirty feeling inside was fading too.

"Out of the question," Mother said when I came downstairs all dressed, hair combed in an unsuccessful swoop over my eyebrow.

We fought about it all through breakfast while the toaster popped nervously. But I'd won in the first moment. The fight was going out of both of them. "Do you want people to see those stitches?" Mother said, playing one last small card.

"Yes, I don't care."

"If you're only going back to defy . . . everybody—"

"I'm going back because I have a right to go back."

Dad didn't make it through breakfast. He went off to pace a floor upstairs. We listened to his footfalls above us while Mother poured coffee over her cup and saucer. "I don't want you to go," she whispered. "I don't want you to be in the same building with—"

"Phil."

"Him. How do you know he won't try something again?"

"At school? I was always safe from him there."

"You're so sure! And I don't want you to have to face that little . . . minx, Alison, who turned on you. Yes, your dad told me every word. I don't want you to have to face any of it. And do you know why?"

"I think so."

"No, you don't. It's because I wouldn't have the courage if I were you. And so I can't understand how you can do it.

"But we couldn't stop you, could we?"

I shook my head and looked down like I was brushing crumbs off my lap. Mother cupped her chin in her hand, tucking her mouth away out of sight.

Dad drove me to school. "If I don't come up with a job pretty soon," he small-talked, "we may just have to sell the house and move back to New York." He spoke of joblessness in a pretty bright tone of voice.

He wanted to walk with me right into school but restrained himself. We sat in the car till the first bell rang, and the tide of kids surged from across the street, slapping books on the car hood, flipping butts, yelling, broad-jumping curbs. The thundering herd. After a week of quiet, I'd forgotten about the unnecessary noise pollution. I leaned over and kissed Dad in the last second and slid out of the car. He was still sitting there when I looked back at the door of the school.

They made way for me when I walked down the corridor, a little like they did for Sonia Slanek. At least I thought so. But it wasn't one big dramatic moment after another. Major scenes you plan for never seem to come along on schedule. Alison spotted me from afar and kept her distance.

I remembered how many times before—say around seventh grade—when I'd vowed never to speak to Alison Bremer *ever* again, over some matter or other. And how we'd be blabbing at each other ten minutes later. That was when we never played for keeps.

Word reached Steve that I was back in school. He was at my elbow by lunch time, silently escorting me a little formally through the cafeteria line. We talked about schoolwork, carefully, across the vast width of the lunch table. Even the salt and peppers seemed significant barriers. I decided he hadn't heard any of the gossip. He always could go deaf around Valerie Cathcart. Did he want me to tell him what he didn't know? I couldn't be sure. "You and Alison have a falling-out?" he asked, out of the blue.

"Yes, a terminal one. Why?"

"Because she just sat down without saying anything. You're practically back to back. They're at the next table."

"They?"

"She and Phil."

Lunch was too long for our short supply of conversation. Valerie skipped around me between fifth and sixth period, suddenly in a mad dash to be somewhere else. But it was a weirdly normal day. By the end of it, I was feeling my way back into the old routine. There were empty spaces in it that Alison had filled. And Steve. But, proud of myself, I skated around these. People spoke, waved, glanced at my stitches. If somebody looked ready to come up for information, I kept moving. People only care within limits.

I didn't have Sonia's . . . visual impact, so I melted into the pack, and besides, I was only last week's rumor. This week had a new topic. The Arts Assembly with Madam Malevich's old movie had made waves—and the local paper. Suddenly Oldfield Village was sitting up and taking notice of its celebrity. The one and only movie theater got hold of three or four of her old flicks and was planning to run them back-to-back in a "Dovima Malevich Film Festival." Posters were plastered all over school.

The next day in drama class, she made no mention of

it. Her hooded eyes skimmed the class as usual, flickering over me with maybe a salute of recognition, then resting on Sonia. She was dressed in a Tyrolean "Heidi" outfit with hair pulled temporarily into braids.

By Wednesday I was hurting. For two days I'd elected not to eat lunch with Steve. One lunch hour in the library. The second at a corner table with a noisy bunch of brown-baggers. I was lonely, but it was too late to go back to bed and be a rape victim. Instead, I pretended that time was passing faster than it really was, urging the weekend nearer. But on Wednesday afternoon the new/old routine came unglued.

Mother'd been conducting a daily countdown to see how fast I'd get home after school. There was no sense in fighting her about it. Maybe in time she'd begin to relax. I wanted to stop by on the way home and see Mrs. Montgomery, only for a moment. Just to reinstate myself as a baby sitter. I wasn't looking forward to more solitary Saturday nights—at the scene of the crime, but I wasn't going to let that cheat me out of my sitting money, or change anything. Nothing was going to cripple me.

"Should you be up and around?" Mrs. Montgomery said. She looked almost shocked when she answered the door.

"I'm fine," I said, bubbling, totally in command, nearly bouncing. I was ready to burst right into her front hall, except that her hand was still on the doorknob.

"Well, come in, Gail," she said, dropping the hand. Angie and Missy were in the living room, watching *Sesame Street* on the set where I'd spent so many hours with *The Late Show*. My eyes flickered over to the fire-place and the brass poker. I couldn't help that.

"Come on back to the kitchen," Mrs. Montgomery said.

"The living room's being occupied by hostile troops." Her house was shadowless and unthreatening during the day. It could have been anybody's. There was still a morning pot of coffee on the stove and the smell of burning from the oven. The kitchen table was swirled with grape jelly. "Not one of my organized days," she said, transferring a pan of black brownies to the sink.

"Let me help—"

"No!" She whirled around and blew a strand of hair out of her eye. "No, I can manage." We stared at each other for a second before she said, "You didn't go back to school, did you?"

"Yes, sure. Couldn't stay home forever."

"No, I suppose not."

The conversation was earthbound. And I needed to start home anyway. "I just came by to say I can start sitting again, on Saturday night."

"I doubt if your mother—"

"I may have a battle there, but—"

"Don't fight her, Gail," she said. "I don't think you should bother."

"Look, if there's one thing I've learned, it's to be careful."

"Yes. Well, so have I." She turned back toward the sink, changed her mind, and came over to sit down across the table from me. "I don't know how to tell you this," she said. "I didn't think you'd *want* to baby-sit any more. It never even crossed my mind."

"Don't tell me you've found somebody else already."

"In this town? Not with my luck."

"Well, then."

"I just don't think it's a good idea, Gail," she said, very fast. "I—I wouldn't be easy in my mind, about you or the kids. After—it—happened, I thought it was all my fault. I felt like an absolute ass going out every Saturday night to that club, carefree as a . . . I almost said a young girl. You're not all that carefree though."

"Let's try it again," I said. "Then if I find out I can't stand being in this house alone with the kids, and you can't stand going out and leaving me in charge, then we can call it off."

She sat there a long time, picking away at a hangnail, letting time pass as if she hadn't already made up her mind.

"I'm sorry," she said finally. "I'd just like to forget it. Phil Lawver—I didn't even mean to mention his name to you—won't get what's coming to him. There'll be no . . . just conclusion to any of this. So what's left but just try to forget it?"

"I don't see how we can."

"Well, I don't mean this to sound harsh. But it happened to you. It didn't happen to me or to . . . Angie or Missy. It's hard enough to raise two little girls all alone even without reminders all the time of what can happen."

"Is that what I am? A reminder?"

"Don't take it personally," she said. "I wasn't ready for this conversation, and so I'm saying everything wrong. Let's just drop it. I appreciate your help in the past, but things are different now."

What could be more final? When I got to the front door, she told me to wait a minute. I thought she'd changed her mind, but she ran back down the hall to dig in a drawer of the telephone table. She came back holding out a closed fist. I was afraid she was going to try buying me off—severance pay. But she dropped Steve's green heart into my hand. When I was walking away down the street under the bare branches, I looked at it and the broken chain.

I walked on, not even trying to see things from Mrs. Montgomery's viewpoint. I was feeling too lost for that. Determined to be so careful all the time, I made it nearly to the end of the block in a daze. I never heard the MG sports car edging up next to the curb, crackling the leaves in the gutter. It was right beside me and braking to a stop when I looked down to see Phil Lawver in the driver's seat.

CHAPTER

Fourteen

"Want a lift home?" he said. It would have been the perfect casual touch if he'd ever offered me a ride before. His pale blue eyes were washed gray by the time of day. My legs tried to buckle. I caught the side of my shoe in a crack of the brick sidewalk, nearly fell, but didn't.

Clenching the heart and the chain, I wondered what kind of weapon they'd be. I began walking faster, planning to outdistance a sports car, I guess. The red hood crept forward, pacing me. "Hey, wait a minute, Gail. What's wrong?"

"I think I can just make it back to Mrs. Montgomery's," I said in a pretty stable voice. "She's at home. She'll hear me yelling before I get to her door. You remember Mrs. Montgomery's house, don't you? It's just back there."

"What's all this about Mrs. Montgomery?" he said in a sensible voice. I forced myself to look at him. His arm in the suede sleeve was resting along the low window. He was guiding the steering wheel with a couple of careless fingers. His blond hair was in shadow, but it looked damp at the ends.

If anybody says or does anything you don't like, yell bloody murder, the lawyer had said. Shall I yell now, I wondered, scream bloody murder into the late afternoon air without a soul in sight? Shall I bring all the housewives defrosting dinners to their small-paned windows? What if you yell and nobody cares? I could picture myself in the distance, screaming my heart out there on the sidewalk, while that nice-looking Lawver boy sat astonished in his sports car.

"Keep away from me, Phil," I said. "I don't think you understand . . . anything. So just keep away."

"I didn't realize." He looked up at me as the car drifted along. "I just didn't realize you were that interested in me. You know Alison and I have this thing going. I can't let anything . . . get in the way of that. Surely you understand."

I crossed the intersection, reeling from that. No traffic unfortunately. Nothing stirred. Even the songbirds had gone south.

"You don't remember, do you? You don't remember the other night," I said, watching where I walked, wondering if that car door might suddenly swing open.

"Which other night?" Phil asked. He was trying to be patient again.

"You don't remember that you raped me."

The wire wheels crinkled through the leaves. "Rape?" he said. "I'd say that was fairly unlikely from both our points of view. I don't have to . . . rape . . . anybody, and you, well, you're pretty open-minded."

"Don't ever come near me again, Phil. I've already seen a law— Just don't ever come near me again." Was I repeating myself? Beginning to babble?

"I can't think why I'd want to," he said. There was just the slightest edge in his voice, cutting the cool.

We were coming up to old Mr. Wertheimer's house. The property nobody could never run across when we were kids, because Mr. Wertheimer had a rock garden out in front with a little flagstone path winding in and out of the marble Cupids and moss roses. Every rock carefully in place.

My hand surprised me by sweeping down and grabbing up one of the border rocks. It was whitewashed, the size of a baseball, heavy as a boulder. The heart and the chain I was clutching fell into the little muddy bowl of earth beneath it.

I whirled around and brought the rock down on the hood of Phil's car. The explosion of stone against smooth sheet metal. The hood latch sprang open. My red reflection creased. I swung the rock sideways then with a discus thrower's might. It crashed against the windshield. A star shape of frosted glass appeared between me and Phil's face. His mouth was open in surprise.

He must have hit the accelerator. The MG jumped forward, and I leapt back, teetering on the curb. He didn't brake for the next corner. The car was a red blur in the gray distance before I caught my breath.

I walked on then. My fingers felt mashed. I'd broken my nails on the car hood. But there was still a lot of fight in me. If that MG had cruised by again, I could have sent the rock through the side window. Oh, I could have done a lot of things. I could have killed.

Just knowing that helped. Knowing I could give Phil Lawver a little hell, even if that only meant scratching his surfaces. Even that much would have been hell for him.

I knew all about Phil then. I felt drunk with all the knowledge. I knew he was missing an important, human part. Call it insanity if you feel like making excuses for him. He thought everything belonged to him and that he could do no wrong. Nobody had ever told him otherwise. At that moment it didn't even chill me to realize how many people there are like that in this world.

But still he was a cripple. When he finally forced himself to prove his virility, he had to stage a horror show to bring it off. Even knocking me out had helped to preserve his privacy.

How scared he must be. How scared he'd always be, always having to forget things he couldn't stand to remember. It was a life sentence, in solitary confinement. He'd be in his house alone, no matter who was there with him.

—What can I say? That thinking this made me feel better? No, but it got me through the moment. I carried the rock from Mr. Wertheimer's garden all the way home, not thinking about the moments to come.

On Saturday night Mother and Dad and I drove through a winterish rain to the Pilgrim Theatre to see the Dovima Malevich Film Festival. The three of us. I hadn't been to a show with both my parents since—when, grade school? Something Disney at Radio City. That little family of ours, once three free spirits, hardly connecting, was still in a huddle. The lights were down when we stumbled in to find three seats together. But I was past caring about being seen out on a weekend night chaperoned by my parents. There weren't any alternatives anyway.

They showed the film we'd seen at school. The thief in the French garden one. And two others a lot like it except that one was a desert picture and the other was set in wartime—World War I, I guess. The men all wore stiff-billed hats and wrappings around their legs. They went to a bombed-out nightclub where Madam Malevich was a dancer, shedding long-fringed shawls and spinning to silent music. She was always the same. Sinuous, young, with worldly eyes working the camera, impossibly slim. She flickered at us in the darkness, and the fairly unruly crowd would lapse into silences, captured by her over and over.

"I just can't believe it," Mother whispered. "Can it really be that same old lady?"

Three films were enough. When the lavender lights came up, people craned their necks, hoping to catch a glimpse of Madam Malevich in the audience. She wasn't there, of course.

It was a full house without her. When we stood up to leave, I caught a glimpse of Sonia Slanek at the end of the front row. I remember that especially because we were both putting on yellow slickers. She even had a red scarf something like mine. But she was better at draping it around her neck. And who knows what exotic costume she had on underneath? She was alone, of course. Then I couldn't see her any more for the black silhouettes all moving to the exits.

They found Sonia the next day, just at the edge of town where Meeting Street becomes the Woodbury Road. She'd been walking home, out to the barn where the sculpture stood in the yard.

When I heard, I pictured her teetering along on the crown of the road in high-heeled boots, lost in her world, enjoying the rain in her face and the dark. Not minding the solitude. Not noticing at first the car lights behind her, the dented hood creeping closer.

I wondered at first if Phil had thought it was me. But I could never know that. And what could it matter to him? The town was full of girls with red scarves and yellow slickers. Or in Levi's or tweed skirts or waitress uniforms. Girls slipping out of cars in parking lots, unlocking front doors, walking home alone from the Pilgrim Theatre. We didn't deserve identity in his mind. We were prey.

That Sunday was cold and bright. A perfect day for weekenders up from New York to tear around the country roads, inhaling real air and scouting for antique shops.

A young couple from Bronxville found Sonia. Somehow they noticed the red scarf in the ditch and the tire tracks on the soft shoulder of the road. They had the wits to stop and investigate.

They brought her in to Oldfield Hospital, thinking she was dead. I imagined her lying in the back of their station wagon, stiff from the cold like a bundle of firewood. She was half strangled by her scarf, people said, and under her slicker her clothes were torn off.

The weekly newspaper carried the story. It doesn't go in for vivid details. The readers add those. It didn't even give Sonia's name, protecting her, I guess, because she wasn't dead. It used the word *assaulted* and moved quickly on to say she was being treated for exposure at the hospital. Her condition was listed as fair. She had pneumonia by the middle of the week. And again I pictured her, under the oxygen tent now, like Snow White in her glass coffin.

The town held its breath—at least the school did— wondering if Sonia would die. Waiting for that moment, suspending judgment. Passing the time by passing the word.

The man who ran the British Imports Automotive

Garage was said to have said that the tire tracks were made by an MG. Somebody said that Sonia was conscious and giving information. Somebody else said she wasn't, that they were keeping her alive on a machine. Valerie Cathcart said the police chief had been seen coming out of the principal's office. Somebody else said that couldn't be right. Nobody ever came out of the principal's office. Not even the principal.

I hadn't been to my locker for a week, not when I knew Alison would be there. We'd worked around each other, and I'd carried a full load of books through all the school days. Suddenly, they were too heavy. I was at my locker after morning classes, and so was she. Our elbows were inches apart, but we pretended we were on separate planets.

Then Steve was there too, taking me by the arm, turning me around. "Do you know who did that to you?" he said in a voice that carried past me to Alison and beyond. "Did you identify him?" We stood there, as close as lovers, and he wasn't letting go of my arm. "I didn't ask you before because I thought you wouldn't want to talk about it. Maybe couldn't talk about it because of the police."

"The police were through with me in the first moment," I said, "but I told them who it was."

Still he didn't let go of my arm. "Do you think it was the same one who did this to Sonia Slanek?" Why is he getting at me now, I wondered, but in a way I knew.

"I think so." And then I turned away from Steve. "Don't you, Alison?"

I'd never seen her run from anything. Not actually pick up her heels and run. She wove through the lunch-hour mob, leaving her locker door standing open.

I closed it for her. People will rob you blind. Even people without needs. "It wasn't . . . was it Phil?" Steve stared past me to the point where the crowd was swallowing Alison up. I could feel what he was feeling. We were still close enough for that. There he stood, a perfectly reasonable, more-than-intelligent human being who hadn't seen the truth because he'd been standing too close to it.

"Yes. It was Phil."

"And you didn't tell—"

"The lawyer told me not to make any accusations I couldn't prove, and there wasn't any proof." My mind swerved quickly among the people I'd told anyway.

"I don't require proof," Steve said. "You should have told me."

"What was the point? You—you might have done something silly. You and I—we were coming to the end of what we had together. That very thing might have— Oh, I don't know."

"Might have forced me to make some grand gesture?"

"Yes. Maybe something like that. What do I know about the male ego?"

"Here's more male ego for you. I'm not quite the well-coordinated jock Phil is. But I could have come up behind him in a dark alley and laid a length of pipe across the back of his head."

"And what good would that have done me?" I said.

"I wasn't thinking about you. You seem to be protecting yourself pretty well by keeping silent. I was thinking of Sonia."

"It's pretty damned easy for you to talk. It couldn't have happened to you."

He dropped his hand from my arm. "In a way, it's happening to us all, isn't it?" he said, and walked away.

It was. I knew that later, when my defenses were down.

If Sonia died or withdrew farther into her shell, Phil would be home free again. There'd be another victim and then another. It was happening to us all. Who was safe, except for Alison, who was in a kind of danger all her own? *Let Alison work that out for herself*, I thought. But I couldn't let it go at that.

I cornered her in the locker room. In a way it was just the right place. She hated gym class. She never liked to sweat.

"Oh for Lord's sake, what do you want," she said when I moved in on her. I had her in a corner. There was nothing behind her but a high wire-covered window.

"You said the other day that if I ever made any waves, you'd go right to Mrs. Lawver," I said.

"Yes, and I meant it. You can't manage to keep that mouth of yours shut, can you?" She was only half into her gym suit. It was true she was never without a bra.

"I just can't please anybody," I said. "Steve's accused me of keeping quiet to make things easy for myself. And you say I talk too much. Maybe you better have the Lawvers run me and my nothing family out of town."

"Oh, why don't you just go of your own accord." She brought up a deep breath and tossed her head. A very bad performance.

"I think you ought to go to Mrs. Lawver, Alison, and have a talk with her. Maybe you can make her understand about Phil. You may just be the only girl in town safe enough to be outdoors by yourself, let alone near his house."

"You've got him all tried and convicted, haven't you— on circumstantial evidence. From what I see on TV you don't get far with that."

"I don't imagine Phil standing trial, not even if I fantasize like crazy. And I don't care much about his tortured soul. But where does it end, Alison? Let's just say that everything you hope for happens. You wave your magic wand, and I disappear from town. Sonia dies. And that leaves you. You and Phil and a town full of girls foolish enough to open doors too quick or walk down lonely roads at night."

"I don't want Sonia to die," she whispered. "How dare you say that? I . . . I don't even want you to leave town. I just want things to be—the way they were before."

"That'll take more than a magic wand, Alison." I gave up on her and walked away. Everyone seemed to be walking away from everyone else that day.

"Gail?" I thought I heard her voice through the clatter of gym lockers and the pounding of the pipes. Why bother turning back? But I did. She stood there, motioning for me to come back, looking from side to side. She looked wretched in a gym suit. Who doesn't?

I came near enough to hear in case she wanted to whisper. Just like the old days, all the way back to middle school. "Listen to me, Gail. I have to say it all at once, or I can't say it at all.

"That night . . . that night Phil came to Mrs. Montgomery's house when you were baby-sitting. Afterward, after he left . . . you there, he came to my house. It was late, but Mother never cares since it's Phil. He . . . there was something wrong with him. He looked terrible. There was something terrible in his eyes. And he was kind of crying. Not really, but almost. It was awful, and he just stood there on the front steps and asked me to forgive him. That's what he said—'Forgive me, Alison,' over and over like a chant. I didn't know what to do. I kept asking him why, what was wrong. But he ran off.

"I thought he was drunk. No, that's not true. I *wanted*

to think he was drunk, or high on something. But I knew he wasn't. I only knew something had happened that I didn't ever want to know about. And then when I heard about you, in the hospital, I still didn't want to know."

"But you did," I said. "You just couldn't let anything spoil all your plans for the future."

"Wait," she said. "Just wait. There's more. On Saturday night Phil and I planned to see those old Malevich movies. It was something to do. But he didn't show up. I sat there all evening, wondering where he was." The tears ran down her face. "I know he's sick. Maybe I knew it before anybody, in little ways, but what was I supposed to do? Maybe you think I'm sick too because a little bit of me blames you and Sonia."

"And do you blame the next victim?"

"Oh no," Alison whispered. "There can't be any more." She shook her head, trying to convince us. We stood there together, like two scared kids. No, that's not it. We stood there like two frightened women.

"What'll I do, Gail? Tell me."

I couldn't. She'd been so sure nothing terrible could touch her. And I'd been so sure when I'd opted out of trying to get Phil arrested. Maybe, working with a lawyer and a lot of luck we could have got him in jail just for one night. Even that might have made the difference.

I don't know if Alison ever went to see the Lawyers. I don't know what she did, or if she did nothing. Whenever we spoke after that, we were both careful never to say anything that mattered.

But there was plenty of talk anyway, and most of the rumors canceled each other out. Some people had it on good authority that a police car had been seen in the

001638g

Lawvers' drive. Or maybe it was an ambulance. Some people said the chief's deputy traced Phil's car to that spot on the Woodbury Road and then got fired for his efficiency. Some people said the Lawvers had let Edna go, and the cleaning woman too, and were living like hermits. It was the first Thanksgiving people could recall that the Lawvers didn't have their reception.

And all the rumors circled closer around Phil until people nodded wisely and remembered the suspicions they'd had all along. But Phil never heard them. There was talk that he'd had a nervous breakdown and was resting in a hospital in Hartford. The last rumor had it that he was captain of the squash team in a boarding school in Vermont. That was the rumor I could believe.

Sonia recovered. But we never saw her again. No more moments of drama in the corridor to break the early-morning school gloom. The Slaneks left their barn and the rusting sculpture behind. Nobody knew where they went. But I think they went back to New York's mean streets where they'd feel safe. It's odd. I miss Sonia as if we'd been friends, even now that I've almost forgotten that Alison and I ever were.

Later, in the winter, Mother said, "It could all have been worse." I guess that was meant to sum everything up, file it neatly away. She'd made her first real-estate sale. It was the Slaneks' barn. A semiartistic family bought it. Mother had her first commission, and so she was looking ahead.

It could all have been worse. I guess she meant that Sonia hadn't died and that her case had shifted attention away from mine. I guess she meant that at least Phil was out of the way. Wherever he was, he didn't come home for Christmas. Maybe she even linked what had happened to the end of that unsuitable, worrisome affair Steve and I had.

"It could have been worse, Mother, but not much." She was sitting at her desk in a little pool of light, composing a real-estate ad for the newspaper. "Not much worse. We were all trying to protect ourselves as individuals and families instead of organizing to make everybody safe. There are more Phils out there, you know."

"Don't talk that way," she said.

"Well, there are. We should have done something else. We still should."

"But what?" Mother said. "What could we do?" And then she turned back to her work.

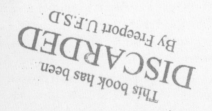